SOMETHING GOOD

The Blisswood Brothers Book 3

EVEY LYON

THE BLISSWOOD BROTHERS

Something Right

Something More

Something Good

Something Beautiful

CONTENTS

About   vii

1. Knox   1
2. Madison   11
3. Knox   20
4. Knox   32
5. Madison   40
6. Knox   48
7. Madison   60
8. Knox   72
9. Madison   81
10. Madison   91
11. Knox   105
12. Madison   118
13. Knox   125
14. Madison   131
15. Madison   139
16. Knox   149
17. Madison   161
18. Madison   168
19. Knox   179
20. Madison   189
21. Knox   199
22. Madison   206
23. Madison   215
24. Knox   224
25. Knox   234
26. Madison   239
    Epilogue: Knox   248

Acknowledgments   255

ABOUT

Knox Blisswood wasn't expecting that his biggest challenge would be something so good...

The first time I meet Madison, she has no idea that I'm the owner of the winery that she just called pretentious, so I play along. The second time, she isn't impressed by my chivalrous act of kindness while I checked out her a... And the third time is the real winner, because Madison mistakes me for my married brother at a parent-teacher meeting–yep, Madison is my little sister's new favorite off-limits teacher. Not only that, but we get thrown together thanks to the high school booster club needing help with an event. My new partner in crime is not a fan of me, and quite frankly, every conversation with her is aggravating. Which is why a simple fact confuses me.

We can't stay away from one another.

We argue and kiss, and I don't want it to stop. The more our lives become entwined, the more I realize that she may just be what I didn't know I was waiting for. But this stubborn woman has to take a chance on us, and although her eyes say yes, her words say no. After all, she has a job on the line. The challenge doesn't deter me, though. Because I'm beginning to feel that Madison and me? We may just be something good...

This enemies-to-lovers romance is the third standalone book in the small town Blisswood Brothers series that follows the brothers as they run their family winery and farm, Olive Owl.

1

KNOX

My fingers tap along the outside of my car door as I drive along the country road, with my other hand on the wheel. Wind softly hits my face from the open window, and I'm enjoying listening to some indie music on the speakers of my pickup truck. Summer has been good to us this year, a constant array of sunshine and warm temperatures. The blue skies and green fields are a contrasting color combo that farmers dream of.

Except I'm no farmer. Well, not exactly.

No, Olive Owl is in principle our family farm and winery. The best in this part of Illinois, which says a lot, as there is a lot of corn around here. However, our place is far too sophisticated to be just a farm. Hell, my brothers and I dress up in perfect buttoned-down shirts every time we have guests at the inn for wine tastings. There is a reason why Chicagoans flood to our place for weekends away.

I'm more than proud of every damn award we have won recently, when it comes to our wine, location, or simply being the best. People say it's the fact that Olive

Owl is run by three brothers that brings an extra bit of charm.

Sure, whatever, I'll roll with that.

I glance into the fields on either side of the road, and it looks like my neighbors are having a good year with their crops too.

My relaxing joyride back from Bluetop—the beloved quirky town that I grew up in—is interrupted by my Bluetooth informing me I have an incoming call. I answer by pressing the button on the steering wheel.

"Knox," my older brother Bennett greets me in a drowsy tone.

"Hey, I'm in the car driving back from the gym. How are things?" I ask as I continue to drive.

"Good… if you enjoy living on a lack of sleep," he quips.

A smirk stretches on my mouth. "That's what happens when you don't use birth control. You end up with a tiny human who sucks all your hours of sleep away," I taunt him in good humor.

Bennett recently became a father… unexpectedly. But he and Kelsey were meant to be, and they are now a family of three and in heaven.

"Yeah, yeah, yeah. Okay, I'm going to swing by the feed store later. Do we need anything else other than Cosmo's last meal?"

"Fuck, stop jinxing us. We all know the day Cosmo trots into his next life that our sister will be devastated," I remind him.

Lucy is our younger sister who entered the scene when I was nine years old, and she is now heading into her senior year of high school. She loves her horse that she got as a birthday gift when she turned six—yeah, calling her the princess of the family is an understatement. Since our mom passed at Lucy's birth and our dad two years ago from cancer, none of us are too keen for her to lose something else.

"I know, but Cosmo is ancient. I'm not sure what super-power he possesses to have lived this long."

I chuckle. "He lives on the sacred ground of Olive Owl, that's what his power is."

"Anyway, Grayson was asking if we can do family night at his new little compound." I can hear the joke in my brother's voice.

Grayson is the oldest of all the Blisswood siblings. He also returned to Bluetop to become Lucy's guardian until she is off to college. Of course, it only took one week back for Grayson to find himself in a romantic situation with his first love, Brooke, who was a single mom. They're now married and all living in a house that Grayson built. He's an architect, so it wasn't just a house that he had built—it is a dream home, complete with swimming pool.

"Yeah, no problem. By the way, are we all going to meet to go over the invoices? We need to do that by the end of the week," I remind my brother.

Bennett and I are the working force behind Olive Owl. Sure, Grayson adds in his opinions and helps when he can, but Bennett and I have only ever known Olive Owl. It's where we began to work as soon as we both finished college where we studied agriculture.

I'm the only one now living on the grounds, as my brothers have their families and wanted to live closer to town because of the kids.

"Dude, I'm coming later today after swinging by the feed store. I needed a *little* sleep to catch up on the lack of, but I'm not that reckless. I know I have responsibilities."

Smiling to myself, I admire that he is juggling it all with a baby and work. "Good to hear. Okay, I'll see you soon. Oh, can you check if the tubing I ordered came in at the hardware store for one of the valves in the barrels?"

"Yep. See ya."

Looking through the windshield, I see that there really isn't a single cloud in the sky today. I make a mental note to check the sprinkler schedule for the coming days when I get home.

As I continue to drive down the empty road, I see a car ahead, pulled over onto the shoulder, but I don't think much about it. When I drive by and look in my rearview mirror, then my foot immediately slams the brakes.

Holy fuck.

Was not expecting that image when I looked in the mirror.

It was only a quick glance, but my eyes picked up the image of a woman leaning against her compact car and looking off into the distance. Her blonde hair gently flowing in the wind and her red-and-white patterned dress the perfect length to flaunt those legs.

No hesitation, I put the truck in reverse, with the wheels squeaking against the road slightly, as if the car is as intrigued as I am right now.

Parking, I review myself in the mirror. People in town say I have model looks, and quite frankly, I have no problem agreeing. Still, might as well give myself the once-over. I'm wearing a white tank that accentuates my muscles and shows my one arm with a little ink which the ladies love. My jeans today are my favorite pair, and to go for the win, I comb my fingers through my wave of brown hair that the sun has lightened.

Opening my door, I slide out of my car and slowly

stride a few steps in the direction of the woman as I swing my sunglasses off.

Her arms are crossed as she leans against her car. She doesn't seem fazed by me and doesn't move as I approach. Instead, she offers me a mere glance.

"Everything alright?" I ask.

Her sapphire-blue eyes meet mine and I have to remind myself to breathe, as she is beautiful—breathtaking, actually. She doesn't wear much makeup, but I can see that her red lips have a fresh coat of gloss or something. The dress that caught my eye, I can now see in great detail, and sweet mother of... the top two buttons are undone.

"Is it really any of your business?" she answers with a shade of sass.

It causes me to grin. "Just trying to be helpful."

"Well, roadside assistance is coming to fix my flat, so I'm already helped. All good." She quirks out her mouth with a breath and looks out into the luscious green field.

Holding my hands up, I try to ease her hesitation toward me. "Will they be long?"

"Listen, *stranger*, I'm fine, so let me stand here and enjoy the sound of silence while I look at these rows of vines." Her hand goes out to display the backdrop.

I lick my lips; I can't leave her now. This angel is appreciating the land of Olive Owl, as we are on the property line. "You're admiring Olive Owl?"

Her head sharply turns to me. "No." She seems to be correcting me. "I hate pretentious farms who think they fit into some chic niche."

The devil. This woman is the devil.

I really want to correct any qualms she has about the family-owned land that is absolutely chic and currently offers delectable-tasting red, but before my words flood out, a thought dawns on me.

She has no clue who I am.

Clearing my throat, I step closer to her. "You've heard of Olive Owl before?" I add, pretend doubt to my tone.

The woman, who seems to be a little younger than myself, scoffs out a breath. "Who hasn't? Isn't that the place that put Bluetop on the map?"

Inside I'm grinning proudly, but I don't let my face show how much her words are perfect to my ears. "Maybe. The high school football team did win state a few years back, could be that."

She tips her nose up slightly, as if she is assessing me, before bringing her hands to her hips, which only accentuates her pert bust that I had to sneak a peek at for a millisecond. "You're from around here?"

I scratch my cheek, knowing I need to play along. "Somewhat. What brings you here? Must have been passing through to be stuck at this location." Then, because I'm cheeky like that, I cock my head to the side slightly. "Or did you secretly want to stock up on pretentious wine?"

"Yeah, overpriced bottles of vino are exactly why I'm stuck in the middle of nowhere." Her sarcasm seeps through her sentence, which causes my upper lip to hitch up. She really does have some strong opinions.

Crossing my arms over my chest, I can't seem to make any effort to walk away.

"But really, just passing through? We notice when someone is new to town. Not only that, but you'll end up with about five hundred casseroles and a welcome committee on your doorstep. And trust me, a suburban millennial who looks like they are in a panic because the nearest outlet mall is thirty miles from here sticks out."

She seems surprised by my words and stands taller as she pushes her body off the car. "Sure, if that's what you think. But I'll have you know, I know how to drive a tractor." A flicker of pride flashes over her face.

My face gives her the *really* look, complete with doubt.

"It doesn't count if it's in an app on your phone."

She flashes me a contrite fake grin. "Anyway. Thanks for checking, but really, you can go now."

"You know, I barely know you, but you seem to be in a shitty mood."

Her eyes grow wide at me. "That's right, you barely know me, and I don't know you. I'm positive the rules of stranger danger apply to both city and flat fields."

I have to grin at this woman who seems a little uptight, the opposite of me, yet I feel a pull to press on.

"Listen, I'm just trying to be a gentleman and make sure you are alright until help comes, but if you prefer to stare off into the prize-winning fields all alone, then fine." I wait for her to have any form of reaction.

I get nothing, so I take that as my cue to turn around and head back to my car, but just as I am about to pivot, she opens her mouth and her cute little tongue darts out to lick the corner of her mouth.

"You're right," she speaks. Raising my brows, I wait for her to continue. "I'm in a shitty mood. I had an interview and I'm not sure how it went. Then I went to get a coffee in town, and it was horrible, almost like poison. Finally, my tire went flat, and I'm stuck against the backdrop of a farm that's the setting for every engagement photo in this corner of the state."

I can't let her last comment go and instead turn to angle my body to her. "You really have strong opinions about Olive Owl. Do you even know much about it?"

"Wow, everyone is very protective of that place, and I don't need to know more."

I don't blink, as she kind of twists me the wrong way, but I can't look away. "It was Sally-Anne's," I blankly say. She looks at me, puzzled. "The coffee. It was Sally-Anne's. Her coffee is fucking tar. Except on Saturdays, you should try Saturdays when the coffee is really good then."

It's really not. It's about ten times worse, but this blonde beauty may need to learn the hard way if she decides to stick around.

"Right." She tucks a loose strand of hair behind her ear. "Well, maybe if I end up here then I will."

My eyes scan her body from head to toe, and she's unreadable but extremely easy on the eyes. "What is it that you do besides criticize local produce?"

She rolls her eyes, annoyed. "I'm very much in favor of shopping local, thank you very much, and it doesn't matter what I do, since you are still a stranger. I don't even know your name."

I lick my lips, debating if I should end this and make her high cheeks flush pink when I inform her who I am, but nah. "I don't know yours either, but it's fine. You can just remember me as the saint that you wouldn't let help you."

"You're no saint." Her eyes narrow in on me and a faint grin plays on her lips. "There is something about you." She steps closer to me, and it causes me to straighten in my posture slightly. "Why don't you be honest with me?" Closer, she's stepping closer, and a rush of blood shoots down my core as her eyes are fixed with my own. She's suddenly turned into an overly confident fox. "You wanted to save the damsel in distress so she would feel so overjoyed with gratitude that maybe you would get lucky."

I scoff a sound and refuse to let this apparently smart

woman win. "No. I stopped as you seem to have lost your way, and you need to head back to where you came from because you seem like a distressed creature out of their habitat."

Her mouth parts open and she shakes her head slightly. "Did you just call me a creature?"

"Did you just assume that you're even attractive enough that I would want to get lucky with you?" I calmly retort.

"*Even* attractive enough?" She continues to shake her head. "Who the hell says that? Besides, we both know that if I was a guy, you wouldn't have reversed to check on me. It only took one glance for you to make a split decision. Guys like you act on looks."

Now my mouth drops low, and my eyes grow bold. This chick has some nerve. "It's not a crime to be good-looking. And for someone who wants to keep me in the stranger category, you have some far-out theories about me."

Both her hands land on her hips and her ass perks out, which makes my brain spin slightly, if that's even possible. "You *are* a stranger!" She raises her voice, and it is beginning to feel like we're bickering.

Knox Blisswood doesn't bicker with women. No, I just have to walk into a room and I'm sure the last thing that 99.9% of the women in the room would want to do is debate with me. My smile has earned me winks, extra muffins at Sally-Anne's, and multiple choices for a good time when I go to Rooster Sin, the local bar, for a drink.

"Well, this stranger is leaving, so good luck with your car." I indicate my head behind her to the car repair truck slowing down as it approaches, before I place my sunglasses back on.

"Swell," she replies without blinking, then with purpose turns her entire body to the man getting out of the truck.

Shaking my head, I walk back to my car, and when I slide into my seat, I feel a little steamed. I've never encountered someone like her who is so tightly strung, the opposite of what I enjoy in a human. And most of all, I'm not used to a woman being a challenge, nor am I sure I could even tolerate her if she told me her name and somehow I run into her again in town. She said she was interviewing here, right? It's all kinds of frustrating.

When I look in my rearview mirror, I catch her staring at my truck, ignoring what the mechanic is saying. It causes the corner of my mouth to stretch, as apparently, I very much enjoy that she isn't unaffected by me.

And with that I drive away.

2

MADISON

I carelessly throw the box of granola into my shopping basket. Although I enjoy cooking, it feels like so much effort when it's only for one person. Normally I meal prep on Sundays for the week, but tonight is Wednesday and I feel like something different than the grilled chicken and veggies that have been sitting in my fridge for a few days.

I blow out a breath. I'm a bit exhausted from the first week of the school year. It's also a new job in a new town, which just means there is an extra element of making impressions and administration to learn. Still, I consider myself lucky that I even have a job as a teacher. Or a job in general. I just graduated from college, along with the millions of other people wanting to start a career. Couldn't exactly get choosey when picking a location, as I have student debt to start paying off.

Yet a small town is exactly what my heart desires, so it was easy for me to look for positions on the map outside of Chicagoland. It reminds me of summers with family, memories I hold dear.

Scanning around the supermarket, it feels pretty empty. Then again, this isn't exactly the suburbs. Every time I've have done groceries since I moved to Bluetop two weeks ago, this store has been lacking people. The few people that I do see are overly friendly and greet me with a smile so wide that it has to hurt.

Assessing my options in the ready-meals section of the deli, I spot a pasta salad and quickly decide that is the winner, so I grab it. Tonight, I'm just going to chill on the sofa and throw on a new series. I have two more days of needing to play nice with the high school kids before I start handing out essays and reading lists. For now, I just want to get to know them and establish myself as a cool teacher.

I think I am nailing this responsible-adult thing. I wear skirts and respectable blouses to work and smile politely when a teenager says something ridiculous. My age makes me just a smidgen over the border of being more understanding than other teachers, as I was a teenager not long ago—I'm relatable.

Right now, I'm in yoga pants post-workout at the gym, with a t-shirt that says *My expectations are based on book boyfriends*, and it's perfect, as I teach English. Plus, I love a good book.

I bring a finger to tap my chin as I contemplate what else I may need. Like a lightbulb going off, I know that I want my favorite snack; chocolate-covered pretzels. The epitome of magnificent, a mix of salty and sweet. I have a bag at least once a week, and normally stash a bag in my classroom in the desk.

Heading down the aisle, I survey all the options until my eyes land on the white-chocolate pretzels on the top shelf and see the empty spot next to them where the milk-chocolate pretzels should be. A glimpse of foil packaging catches my eye, and I realize there is still a bag that must be stuck at the back of the shelf.

I'm not petite nor tall, but I bend over to place my basket on the ground and then stand on the bottom shelf and reach my hand up. My fingertips barely touch the bag, and even my determination for my snack isn't enough to distract me from the realization that someone is watching me.

Glancing over my shoulder, I quickly do a double take when I see that the man has his head tipped and he seems to be looking at my ass that admittedly is a little pert in these pants.

But it isn't just *a* man. It's *the* man.

"You!" I nearly hiss and hop off the shelf.

"Hey, stranger." His cheeky grin is undeniably sexy, and I would blush if it weren't for the fact that this man is an asshole.

The guy from a few weeks back when I had a flat tire. It was already a bad day after my interview went horribly—as in I spilled coffee on the principal, and I didn't seem to answer anything correctly. Then my wandering through Bluetop was a mix of excitement that this place is cute and livable to freaked out because there was no decent coffee. To top it all off, this man stopped on the side of the road like I was candy he could so easily have if he smiled.

Overconfident men irritate me.

Men with cutting jawlines, gorgeous hair, who wear tight white tank tops, with hard muscles and a tattoo which maybe gives an inkling that he has a rugged persona going for him. Plus, men who look like Chris Isaak *Wicked Games* era, they just darn right infuriate me.

My hip tips out and my hand finds my waist. "Were you checking out my ass?"

Fuck, I did not just say that.

"And if I was?" He seems satisfied, not concerned, that I caught him. Then he has the audacity to reach up and with one sweep grabs the pretzels off the shelf. "I'm a perfect gentleman." He continues to grin as he holds up the bag of pretzels and shakes it as if he has the prize.

And he does.

"Can I have those?" My hand motions for him to pass them to me.

"No please?" He flashes his eyes to me.

I grumble from his demeanor. "*Please* can I have the pretzels?"

He looks between the bag and me, pretending to debate, then he tosses them into my basket.

"Uptight girl, you're back." He leans against the shelf and magically avoids knocking anything over, as he somehow has mysterious powers.

Licking my lips and looking around, I see that we are alone. "I am."

"Got the job?" he says, attempting to make conversation.

"I did."

I do my best to avoid meeting his gaze. Admittedly, he is a bit too smoldering on the eyes for me, and although people generally consider me a nice person, this man brings out the worst of me. It's as if my body short circuits at the sight of him and I become someone unrecognizable.

Clearing my throat, I straighten my posture and hold my basket close to my stomach, realizing that I am wearing an outfit that must make me look completely disheveled.

"You can handle small-town life?" He continues his line of questioning with his smirk never fading.

My mouth opens as I want to challenge him, but I remind myself that I'm in public. Instead, I swallow my retort. "Actually, yes. Believe it or not, I used to spend summers living with my aunt and uncle who have a farm down near Peoria."

His eyes grow wide, and he propels off the shelf. "Really? Well then, guess I was wrong about you, short-cake. Or am I right and you just somehow got stuck here… again." He winks at me.

"Not stuck," I correct him. "Here of my own free will, and everyone in Bluetop seems lovely, except for the guy who has now checked me out twice."

"We never established if I was checking out your ass or not. Besides, I helped you get your pretzels, I'm just being chivalrous." He pretends to touch his heart.

I scoff a laugh because this man is unbelievable. "I'm sure you deserve a trophy," I say, sarcastic.

He chuckles under his breath. "Oh, I will definitely collect it." His eyes scan me from head to toe and my entire body comes alive with heat.

I wasn't volunteering myself as the prize, but there are worse things.

"Anyway, I should go." I try to avoid our eyes locking and take a few steps, but he blocks me by standing in the way.

"Don't you want to introduce yourself?" He looks at me, amused.

I confidently shake my head no. "With the guy who makes poisoning myself seem like a good option? No." I brush past him, touching his shoulder in the process, and it causes a zap of electricity to shoot inside of me, and I begin to walk away.

"Yikes, you should destress a little. I hear the wine aisle

is having a sale on Olive Owl wine. I'm sure you will love that," he calls out.

I don't dare look back to see how much he enjoyed our little dealings in the chip aisle.

A man distracting me while I attempt to become a good teacher is not what I need, I remind myself.

———

POURING myself some coffee in the teacher's lounge, I smile at my colleague, Ellie. She's a few years older than me, recently married, and teaches algebra and calculus. Right away, we hit it off as we started the school year.

"Thanks for bringing this banana bread," she mumbles with a mouth full of baked goods that I made myself. "We still have blueberry muffins left from Monday that you brought."

My shoulders raise toward my ears. "It's okay, I had the time. Plus, it's my pleasure. Something for my new colleagues." I smile brightly at her.

Truthfully, I have spare time, as my social life is lacking at this moment, and I want to make a good impression on my colleagues. "How many parent-teacher meetings do you have left today?" I ask her before I sip from my mug of coffee that says *Commas are our friends*.

Bluetop High has a program that is actually kind of cool. Every senior is partnered with a teacher and that teacher guides them through their next steps after graduation. Instead of having a guidance counselor, the teacher helps the student with college applications or job searches, anything really.

Today we meet with the parents of our students.

She pulls her dark hair up into a ponytail. "Two more, and you?"

"One. Lucy Blisswood's brother."

From the one week of school so far, she's been my favorite student. Smart, funny, and she has potential to go to a good college which is what she has stated that she wants.

"Oh, Grayson is nice. He moved back when their dad passed, to be Lucy's guardian. He got married recently too. Actually, he married his high school girlfriend. They were both Homecoming king and queen together. Cute, huh?" Ellie is a Bluetop native, so she knows her facts.

"Didn't he just have a baby?" Margaret, the art teacher, mentions as she walks into the teacher's lounge, adjusting her glasses. She's about to retire soon.

"Nah, that's Bennett, the other brother," Ellie corrects her.

Moving out of Margaret's way, I smile to my colleagues. "Look, I should probably run, as I have this meeting. We have the booster club meeting right after, right?"

Margaret laughs humorously, yet it kind of scares me. "Oh, we do. With the parents and the dictator too."

"Dictator?" I'm puzzled.

Ellie cuts in. "Yeah, Helen. She used to have kids who went here like ten years ago, and she has refused to give up her spot as president of the club, and she has this little hammer to keep the meetings in order. To her credit, she keeps everything moving and raises a bunch of money for the school."

"Okay, anything else I need to know?" I ask as I stand in the middle of the room holding my mug.

"Nah, good luck with your meeting," Ellie answers, and with that, I smile then head out.

———

A FEW MINUTES LATER, I'm in my classroom and decide to clear the whiteboard while I wait. I've already thought about which timelines I need to give to Lucy and her brother for applications and which books will help her with her college essays. These meetings are actually without students, which is great, as I can maybe find out the home situation or if there is something I need to be worried about or consider.

My last parent-teacher meeting, I discovered quite quickly that the dad was pushing their son to compete in minor league baseball, while the mom doubted if that was the right choice, as their son has expressed an interest to join the military.

It's these little *ah-ha* moments that help puzzle these teenagers' lives together.

My excitement for the day comes out through humming a Taylor Swift song. As I finish erasing the board, I see a flicker of movement in the corner of my eye, which means Grayson Blisswood has arrived for our meeting.

With a smile wide on my face to greet him, I set the eraser down. "Good afternoon, Mr. Blisswood."

I turn around, only for my smile to fade when I realize that for the third time, I've come face to face with the mysterious man who shows up in my dire times of need, when I may have been stuck with white-chocolate pretzels instead of milk chocolate.

"Well, well, well, you must be Madison Roads then, my little sister's new favorite teacher. No longer a stranger."

He grins as he strides into my classroom before he sits on the chair I set out in front of my desk, leans back, and sips his to-go coffee from Bear Brew—the good coffee in town and not Saturday coffee at Sally-Anne's like this monster suggested—and he seems to be enjoying the view.

My jaw drops because he looks good, in a black t-shirt with dark blue jeans. But I'm not allowed to think that. No. Not at all. Because he's married! Yes, that's what Ellie mentioned.

Oh no.

I knew he was trouble. Grayson Blisswood has been checking me out when he has a new wife at home.

"You're fucking unbelievable," I utter as I begin to fume.

He looks taken aback, but I don't care. There is no way I'm going to let him off the hook.

3

KNOX

Did this vixen actually just curse at me?

Her name is Madison. I know this because Lucy, my sister, hasn't stopped talking about her new English teacher. The teacher that I am supposed to meet because my brothers can't.

Me, Knox Blisswood, somehow got roped into the responsible-older-brother role of ensuring our kid sister is ready for her senior year of high school. I'm the brother who wants to ensure that Lucy enjoys her senior year and knows she has options, and if she doesn't want to do the college thing, then I will shut that train down right now, even if my brothers don't like it.

This is the meeting I wasn't overly excited about, but now I think I fucking struck gold.

Except Madison Roads looks like she may kill me.

She points a finger at me and begins to rant. "You're married and you flirt with other women. Unbelievable."

My face must turn puzzled, as I'm not sure why she thinks I'm married.

"Look, Grayson, I—"

I quickly cut her off by standing up and holding my palm up. "Hold it there, horsey, let me stop you right there. I'm not Grayson."

It dawns on me that we never informed the school that I'd be coming in place of Grayson.

"But if you're not Grayson..." She tries to understand and calms for a second before her jaw drops again. "Unbelievable. You have a newborn baby and you—"

I interrupt her again. "Also, not me. That's Bennett, my other brother."

Madison looks completely confused. "Then who are—"

Grinning, I sit back down and confidently lean back and throw my feet up on her desk. "Knox, the brother with the devilish good looks who is neither married, has a kid, or is even tied to anyone, which is what I am sure you wanted confirmation on." I sip my coffee casually as the news sinks into her.

Her fingertips rest on the desk that she towers over as she looks at me. An O shape forms on her beautiful mouth. "I... I... didn't realize Lucy had another brother. Nobody mentioned you in the teachers' lounge."

My hand finds my chest. "That wounds me. I'm the best Blisswood around." I'm a little cocky, but it's all in good jest. "Grayson is on a delayed honeymoon with his wife, a hurricane ruined their timeline, and Bennett's kid has chicken pox, so... surprise, here I am." I bring my arms out like I'm on display.

"Oh," she says simply before straightening her forest-green blouse that is supposed to be respectable, but Christ, it hugs her tits. Her hand runs down the fabric to straighten her pencil skirt. This woman was made to look like a teacher who I've been fantasizing about since I was fifteen.

Madison drops onto her chair and clears her throat.

"I apologize for… my… misconception." I can hear the struggle to get that out.

"Of today or in general?"

She rolls her eyes then offers me an overdone closed-lip smile. "I see you're enjoying the *good* coffee, or is it because it isn't Saturday at Sally-Anne's?" She raises a brow at me.

My tongue glides around my mouth in pleasure from the fact that she took my misguided advice.

"Oh dear, you actually listened. Did you go before or after reading Mr. Darcy, your book boyfriend?"

I can tell by her face that she remembers the fact that I saw her in a fucking adorable t-shirt about book boyfriends. "Wow, he has a brain or at least knows the name of one of the greats. But I'm positive you are more a Wickam or Laurie—cold and heartless."

"Hey, as long as it's Christian Bale's version of Laurie."

Her entire face turns surprised that I just said that. "You know Little Women?"

I don't answer her, as I kind of enjoy that her mind has just been blown. I won't tell her that I knew these characters purely because I read an article the other day about literature that makes women turn frisky that was crammed between an article on food and the sports scores.

Tipping my head with a satisfied smirk, I taunt her. "Uh-oh. Is your mind about to explode from the fact that my looks and literature knowledge combined are all your fantasies rolled into one?"

Her lips curl into her mouth, and I can tell she is fighting not to say something, because I think I just pressed her pissed-off button again.

Instead, she shakes her head as if she needs to snap out

of distraction. "Now, shall we focus on your sister, Mr. Blisswood... Wait." She stops again in thought.

"Please don't call me Mr. Blisswood, it isn't good for my brain." Because when she says it, it sounds like a purr right before she could do something naughty that I would thoroughly enjoy.

Madison studies me for a second, then her jaw flexes side to side. "Blisswood... so *you* own the winery."

"With my brothers, yes." *Ah, I see the dots have finally connected for her.* "We produce pretentious award-winning wine." I throw my empty cup of coffee like a basketball into the trash bin without batting an eye as I stare at her.

Her face turns a perfect shade of pink, but she brushes past my quip. "Shall we focus on Lucy, Mr.—" She closes her eyes and gathers a breath. "Knox."

I enjoy hearing my name on her lips, it nearly lingers in the air.

Madison begins to look at some papers on her desk, and for a moment I would swear she is flustered. "I think it's best that we plan a deadline for October if she really wants to make early admission. If we stick with October for Lucy to have all of her college essays complete, so that I can review them before she submits them November first. I understand she would like to go into liberal arts, which is perhaps why Principal Beal paired us together. She mentioned Hofstra, Syracuse, and also Northwestern here in state. All great schools—"

I stop her spiel because she already lost me at college essays. "Look, Madison, I'm just going to lay it out there. As much as my brothers are excited that Lucy is doing so great in school and wants to go to college, I view it all differently."

Her eyes finally peer up to meet my own. "How so?"

"She'll burn out if she keeps trying to ace every quiz and follow the path she thinks she is supposed to," I explain as I lean back in the chair. "Sometimes I think she should take a year off and go travel through South America or somewhere. The last few years were intense enough."

A wave of what I can only describe as sympathy washes over Madison's bright face. "I'm sorry, I understand that you lost both your parents."

"Our mother, Lucy doesn't remember. And our dad not long ago, yet Lucy moved on like nothing happened. Maybe we all did."

She nods slowly in understanding. "I see where you're coming from, and college isn't for everyone. Hell, I'm not even sure how far a degree gets you these days, depending what field you want to get into. There are literally sixteen-year-olds posting a viral video and then making millions. If Lucy expresses she wants a different path, then that's fine, but the first day of school she asked me about helping her with her college applications, and that's what I intend to do."

I went to college per my father's insistence, and it wasn't all that bad. "I'm not against college, I had a grand ole' time in Sigma Epsilon."

A sound of disbelief escapes her mouth. "You were a frat boy?"

"Does that surprise you?" Kind of surprised me too, but the parties were good.

She seems to be assessing me with her eyes as she plays with a pen in between her fingers. "Yes, actually."

I cock my head to the side. "See, Maddie, that's why you shouldn't jump to conclusions. You may have me all wrong."

Madison folds her arms against her body. "Trust me,

frat boy isn't a step up in my esteem. Shall we just keep it to the point and discuss how you were checking out my ass at the supermarket?"

"Now is this a professional conversation to have with the equivalent of a parent to one of your students?" I chastise her with a grin.

"I don't care who you are, but I will always call someone out for being a jerk, and that's what you were, all ogle-eyed." She seems to be fired up again.

"You know, I'm a little concerned that you are my sister's guidance counselor or buddy, whatever the hell Principal Beal calls this setup. The last thing I want is Lucy to be influenced by a woman who thinks sniping at a gentleman for being helpful is ultimate goals."

The sound of her chair screeching against the floor fills the room as she pushes her chair back and stands. "No, teaching her that a *stranger* approaching her with a grin and eyes that clearly were searing over my body *can* be called out."

"I was searing over your body? Is that even a sentence? You teach English, right?"

She grumbles or growls, I'm not quite sure, but this is entertaining.

"Look, how about we just agree that I will e-mail Grayson the deadlines and proposed suggestions of books to read, then call this meeting closed." She breathes out a long sigh.

Looking at my watch, I realize that, as much as I want to drag this out for kicks, I've been summoned to another task that somehow my brothers and I got roped into. "Fine. I have the booster club meeting anyway, and Helen will be none too pleased if I'm late."

"Shit." Her hand comes to her forehead. "Forgot about that."

"Oh, yeah?" Now I'm intrigued. "Have you been volunteered as tribute since you're the newbie?"

"Yes. I have to help out, but it's fine, as it's not like I'm too busy—" She seems to catch her sentence, then her words drag. "I mean, I'm sure I can squeeze in the time to help."

Huh, I think she just let it slip that she is single and one of those bookworm people who wears fuzzy socks with mugs of tea in hand. Truthfully, it didn't cross my mind that she may have a boyfriend, and for some reason it wouldn't stop the urge I have to rile this woman every time I see her.

"I can walk you to the auditorium if you want, or is that going to ruffle your feathers again?" I stand and look at her for an answer.

"I think it's better if we go our separate ways. I feel like a headache erupts every time we meet, and I don't know why," she quips, and it only makes me smirk.

"See? We are made for one another because I feel the same."

She just rolls her eyes at me before we both head to the hall and she goes her separate way.

———

STANDING against the back wall of the auditorium, I listen to some irate mom complaining that the cheerleaders' skirts are too short. Before that, a dad was requesting more money for the science club so they can go to some robot competition downstate.

Typing on my phone with my thumb, I text my brothers

in our group chat, although I hope for the sake of his honeymoon that Grayson doesn't respond.

Me: Lucy's English teacher is a piece of work.

Bennett: What do you mean?

Me: She's the woman I told you about from the side of the road. Feisty, grumpy, has it out for me. A judgmental shrew, really.

I get a gif of a laughing raccoon.

Bennett: So she isn't an old lady who teaches Shakespeare?

Me: Nah, just graduated from college, I think. Are we sure we shouldn't ask for a new buddy for Lucy? Maybe someone with more experience and who doesn't chew my head off?

Grayson: NO! Don't do that. Lucy already said she's happy, and we need her stress-free during college applications.

Bennett: Go back to your honeymoon

Grayson: We're on a break

I cringe. He inserts a winking emoji.

Bennett: Fuck, TMI.

Me: Okay, so we want our sister to be influenced by a moody teacher?

Bennett: Are we talking about the same person? Lucy says great things.

I insert an annoyed emoji because I shouldn't be getting so much resistance on this topic.

Grayson: I'm sure she will be professional, so do me a favor and suck it up. By the way, I told Helen to count on Olive Owl to help with the fundraiser.

Helen coincidentally also helps us out at Olive Owl, more running the inn when we have guests than anything.

Me: I would know what we've been roped into on

the responsibility train, except I've been listening to high-strung parents debating forever over ridiculous requests. Someone mentioned peanuts in the lunchroom and all hell broke loose until Helen reined us all in.

Grayson: With her little hammer?

Me: Last time I do this.

The movement in the corner of my eye causes me to glance up, and I see that Miss Bothered-and-Prim is arriving late to this meeting.

"Tsk, tsk, Maddie, I believe you have been playing hooky," I berate her as I slide my phone back into my pocket.

Her audible exhale informs me that she is annoyed that we're meeting so soon again.

"Wasn't playing hooky. Had to deal with an issue," she whispers loudly. "But I can hear that little wooden hammer all the way from the teachers' lounge. Is it really neces-sary?" She crosses her arms as she looks forward but leans against the wall.

"Some people here need to be kept in line." I give her side-eye, and she looks at me and offers me another fake smile of hers that makes me believe she finds me funny but can't let me know.

"Knox!" The sound of a table being knocked on feels like background noise, as Madison and I seem stuck in a moment where neither one of us can look away. "Knox Blisswood, yoo-hoo."

Helen's high-pitched tone causes me to draw a line from Madison to the front of the room where Helen is sitting behind a table with Coach Dingle, who was close with my dad, and Principal Beal, who looks at me with adoration because she just has a soft spot for former students. Helen's permed hair and sweater with some sort of cat figure on it causes me to remember how serious she takes her role.

"Yes?" I nearly croak out, as I fear what is about to come.

Helen claps her hands together and her smile is too wide for my liking. "You will be okay organizing the stall for Homecoming? It's for the booster club fundraiser. I mean the logistics? We could use some strong arms to help hammer in some nails. We have a lot of hard wood to get through to make the stall."

I hear Madison choke on a chortle and then pretend to clear her throat. Apparently, Helen's innocent sentence was enough innuendo for Madison, and also the few moms who are suddenly throwing me sultry gazes.

I need to get out of here stat.

"Sure. My brothers and I can help." I smile awkwardly.

Helen takes a pen and crosses off her list. "And Grayson mentioned that we could use Olive Owl for the teacher-appreciation dinner."

"Fine." I don't give it much thought, as I want us to wrap up this meeting.

Madison leans in and speaks to me in a low voice. "Heartfelt."

"And you, Ms. Roads, can help him," Helen adds. "I'm partnering you with Knox for all efforts with the dinner and Homecoming. Maybe you're good with tools too and can help Knox with nailing things together." Helen proudly crosses off her list, completely unaware of her choice of words. I swear I hear mumbles, just like Coach who is shaking his head into the palm of his hand.

Madison shakes off the image that I'm sure she is contemplating, of pounding my wood, and gets to the point. "M-me?" she stammers out. "What do you mean?"

"Of course, dear, it's tradition for the new teacher to help arrange the dinner and help at Homecoming. We always partner a parent with teacher to ensure we conquer our to-do list, and you still haven't been assigned anything… until now."

Madison's finger comes up to indicate between herself and me. "Me and Knox?" I hear the uneasiness in her voice.

"Mmhmm."

"I don't think I need help," I throw in.

Helen blinks a few times. "Of course you do, and it's tradition."

"I'm sure there must be some other to-do thingy that I can do." She's trying to weasel her way out of this.

"Wow, thingy. Big words, teacher," I tease her through a loud whisper only she can hear.

"Nope. That was the last of the items," Helen declares before hammering once to adjourn the meeting. "Thank you, everyone."

Very quickly noise circulates in the room as parents stand to leave. I turn all my attention to Madison who almost has a sour face on, while her hand slides to the back of her neck to try and soothe the fact that there is no escape.

"Fucking fantastic," I softly mutter, but she hears.

"Aren't you only the fill-in tonight? I mean, your older brother is back from his honeymoon soon, so…"

"Nice try, but I already agreed to help him out with this. Plus, it's for Lucy."

"Of course," her tone goes soft.

Looking around, I swear Sophie Plums just winked at me, despite her husband walking a few strides behind her.

Helen shimmies on past us. "Don't forget to exchange

numbers so you can discuss logistics," she calls out in passing and wiggles her fingers in the air.

I grin at Madison. "Guess you're handing over your number. You know, for all that... *hammering* we need to do."

Her eyes snap to my direction with a sharp glare. "Let me watch paint dry before that happens."

"Oh, but it may happen?"

She grumbles in frustration as she reluctantly hands me her phone so I can type in my number. Then I call myself before handing back her device. Pulling my phone from my pocket, I wiggle it in the air at her.

"Lucky me," I tell her in a dull tone.

"The luckiest," she snipes before she pivots and fades off into the distance.

My arm hooks right then left as my friend Drew ducks under then sideways. We're boxing in the backyard at Olive Owl, as we always do twice a week. Sometimes we go to the gym, but the weather has been too great not to work out outside.

Drew is a few years older than Lucy and a few years younger than me, and when he was in a hard spot, Grayson suggested that Drew come work for us. It was a great decision because Drew has a knack for building things and helping with hard labor at Olive Owl. He's also a cool guy to hang out with and the perfect sparring partner.

"You okay, man? You seem a little tense," he informs me through heavy breathing and blocking my uppercut.

I use a little extra force to hit the pads he's using to block my movements. "Nah." I brush it off like he's crazy.

After my final swing, we throw off our boxing gloves to drink from our water bottles and towel off our sweat.

"I had one of those parent-teacher meetings for Lucy. Her teacher is, ugh…" I scratch my chin as I consider how to describe the woman who is taking residence in my thoughts rent-free. "Interesting."

"You mean hot?" Drew calls me out. He stares at me and takes another chug from his bottle.

"I mean, she is easy on the eyes, but her scornful personality makes me wonder if she lives near the earth's core and spends Thanksgiving with the devil because they're neighbors. Positive she fucking hates me too." And why does that excite me? I really do not know.

He holds his hand up to stop me. "It *really* bothers you."

"W-what?" My voice goes a little high, which just gives me away.

Drew waves a finger at me. "Yeah, you want her to like you. Or rather, you're not used to a woman making it so difficult for you. That's it, isn't it?" He grins confidently.

Throwing my stuff into my gym bag, I don't give his hypothesis any further thought. "I'm sure I could win her over with the snap of my fingers," I assure him, but inside I have serious doubts, because Madison seems like she would make me grovel and only then would she even bat her lashes at me.

"It must be hard, having every available woman in this town ready to claw you down into commitment, but the one you may actually turn your head for fucking hates you. Classic." Drew seems to take pleasure in my situation.

"I'm not saying I'm into her."

"Into what?" My sister's voice breaks into our conversation as I whip my head to the right to see Lucy walking over to us without even glancing up from her phone as she swipes on the screen. Her blonde hair is in a braid to the side and her jean shorts and boots informs me she went to see her horse.

"Um, into… which new bottles to buy for the next barrel of olive oil that will be ready soon," I lie.

Drew looks at me humorously because me lying means I'm trying to hide something, which in turn means that I have something I don't want Lucy to know. Such as her teacher is an insufferable goddess.

Lucy looks up at me with a peculiar expression. "Oh, didn't think you cared about that stuff." True, as I let Bennett handle the marketing side of the business. "Listen, I fed Cosmo and cleaned his stall, but can you check on him later? I feel like he's lonely or something. Like that's a thing, right?"

I shake my head. "I mean, I guess."

"Oh, and how was Ms. Roads?" she asks excitedly, and it's refreshing to see her face light up in relation to school.

"Yeah, how was she?" Drew flashes his eyes at me.

I nervously laugh under my breath. "It was a… fruit-ful… meeting," I drag out a sentence.

"Okay, and? What did you discuss?" Lucy is waiting for me to divulge further details.

Looking between Drew and Lucy, I decide to just keep it as simple as can be. "Not much, you know, the usual. Literature, deadlines, essays. She seems like a real delight." I throw on a tight smile.

"You didn't discuss my approach to college applications? Or how I'm excited that we're going to focus on *The Great Gatsby* in class? Did she mention my contri-butions to the group on our first day?" Lucy lists and crosses her arms, waiting for more information.

I glance to Drew who is also waiting patiently for my answer. "You know, she just said it would be easier to e-mail Grayson with all the info."

Lucy groans and her shoulders drop, as she seems

slightly aggravated. "What was the point of you being sent to the meeting then? Did you do something? It's you, of course you did. Tell me she doesn't hate me now through association."

"Hey!" I'm slightly offended. "I did absolutely nothing… at the meeting." *Other times may be questionable.* "We were short on time because of the booster club." My tone turns upbeat as I think I may turn my sister's mood around. "Good news. I'm helping with the staff-appreciation dinner with your favorite teacher, *and* the Homecoming game." I even add a little fist pump in the air.

"What?!" she shrieks. "No, please no." She shakes her head. "For once, I'm excited about a teacher, and I really feel like your asshole tendencies may ruin this. And I can say that, as it's coming from a place of love and honesty in my heart."

I pinch the bridge of my nose between my fingers, as I'm not sure how to take the fact that my sister holds me in such little regard or that she is so comfortable with me that she can be openly honest.

"Duly noted. Now, shall we go grab some lunch? The newlyweds are back soon, and I won't be able to eat once they enter with their cutesy stuff."

"I'll see you all a little later, I want to go check on the field to the west." Drew waves us off, and I can't help but notice my sister's eyes following his path.

Waving a hand in front of her face, she blinks a few times and then focuses on me.

"Okay there?" I ask.

She hums in response.

Touching her arm, I feel we can have an honest moment since she isn't shy to hide away her opinions about me. "Senior year is kind of big."

"Yeah, and?"

"Lucy, you're only young once, don't burn yourself out. Enjoy planning a senior prank or something. As much as I love how you outsmarted all of us in grades, only do this college stuff if it's really what you want."

For a split second, I could swear she may agree, but just as fast, her face turns neutral. "It is, I mean, my plan and my choice."

Even though I doubt her, I play along with this. "Okay. We can plan a graduation trip then somewhere. You and me, no married siblings."

Every brother has a soft spot for Lucy in their own way. A sort of connection that is a cross between older brother and something more due to the age difference and what we've all been through, losing our dad. My connection is that we can joke with one another, prank the others, and share an understanding that I will keep her intel to myself when she tells me what someone did at some secret high school party the weekend before.

Truthfully, I will miss her when she heads off to college. She and I are the ones not tied down and observe our brothers' new families from the sidelines.

"I'm so relieved that they found a new teacher over the summer. I was so stressed that I would be under the watchful eye of Mrs. Stevens who is an absolute pain. But luckily, she decided to follow her husband to Florida for early retirement. Ms. Roads seems super chill."

I clear my throat. *Super chill* is the last thing I would describe Madison as, unless we are describing her heart. I nod awkwardly. "Do you even know much about her?"

"Sure. She is from the suburbs of Chicago, but I have some strange feeling that she doesn't really mind it all the way out here. Just graduated from U of I, and she thinks

Sense and Sensibility is way better than *Pride and Prejudice*. Plus, she always has chocolate pretzels on her desk."

"You've been back, what, a week, two weeks, and you get all of this?"

Lucy touches her braid and shields the sun from her eyes with her other hand. "Yes, I need to know who I'm dealing with if she's writing me recommendations for applications."

"I'm sure we can work our Blisswood charm on that one."

"Or not. Ugh. You, Bennett, and Grayson really need to get over the ego trip you all have. We are not Bluetop royalty." She begins to walk away, clearly done with this conversation.

A doubtful sound escapes me. "Not sure I agree." I mean, we do contribute a lot to the community, Sally-Anne never makes me wait in line at her bakery, and everyone still mentions Olive Owl's full-page spread in a few travel magazines a few years back.

We begin to walk toward the main house that serves as the inn and my home. Lucy partly turns to me and points a finger at me. "You've been warned. Please don't do anything to piss off my teacher."

Holding my hands up in defeat, I accept the fact that my sister would kill me if I do anything that would remotely unsettle the waters with her English teacher who wears hot-as-fuck pencil skirts and causes my cock to twitch from a mere scowl.

I exhale a long breath. I need a cold shower.

———

TEXTING Madison Roads later after my shower is probably not what Lucy had in mind when she told me to behave. But, you know, we need to sort out logistics in a professional manner. Holding the towel knotted around my waist, I type in my other hand.

Me: Am I disturbing or are you and your book boyfriend on a break?

Hot pepper, fire, devil emoji.

I throw my phone onto my bed as I grab a shirt from my drawer, only to hear the ping come right back at me. Because I'm instantly excited, I pick up my phone in record time.

Madison: Funny. Must be such an ego killer that women enjoy fictional men more than being in your company.

Me: Must be such a disappointment that your one-off dates always end on page 362 of your e-reader.

Madison: So, to what do I owe the pleasure? Couldn't find someone else to piss off on this fine Saturday?

Me: Actually, contrary to your misguided thoughts in relation to me, I believe we have to arrange some quality time together for the sake of the young impressionable kids.

She types, then deletes, and types again. Meanwhile, I drop onto the bed and lie on my side, wondering what retort she will come back with.

Madison: Sure, let me stock up on my pepper spray and mentally prepare myself for boredom.

Me: So that's a "yes, Knox, I would love to come to your chic and sophisticated winery that everyone raves about"?

Madison: I guess I have no choice. What is it that I am supposed to do? Screw you?

Me: Wow, to the point.

Madison: Screwdriver. I meant screwdrive things together. We are supposed to build something, right?

I insert a thinking emoji.

Me: Yeah. Not much better... So, do you want to bang out this list tomorrow or during the week when you're hopped up on stress from all that teenage angst?

Madison: Tomorrow. During the week I help with the drama club.

My head tips side to side at that image.

Me: So, you like to roleplay?

She sends me back rolling eyes.

Madison: After lunch tomorrow? I have a brunch thing in the morning.

Me: Sure, that will give me enough time to consider being on my best behavior.

Madison: Hope your brain can handle that thought process. It must hurt when you think beyond yourself.

Me: Geez, tomorrow will be a real treat.

Madison: Wow, we may actually agree on something, and I'm not even sure hell has frozen over yet. Goodbye, Knox.

Me: Goodbye, Maddie.

I don't need to look in the mirror to know that I have a goofy grin on my face from a woman who actually has wit, looks, dislikes me so much that it interests me, and sadly should be off-limits.

All the attributes that make me completely want to wind her up until she comes undone underneath me.

And who am I not to take on the challenge?

5

MADISON

Sally-Anne's is buzzing, with people talking over their Sunday brunch, as every table is full. This place isn't fancy by any means, and the coffee is in fact horrible, to which everyone is well aware of, except Sally-Anne herself, but man, she makes a good coffee cake, and her sandwiches rock too.

Ellie smiles brightly at me as she stirs a packet of sugar into her iced tea. "You look really cute today. The light blue really highlights your eyes. Is this how you always look on a Sunday?" She peers down at her own outfit of yoga pants and a loose gray shirt since she just came from the gym.

I brush off her compliment and tilt my shoulder up. "It's just a blouse and jeans."

"Okay, sure. Want to go for a walk after this, down by the river?"

Finishing my bite of cherry coffee cake, I say, "Can't. I have booster club duty and need to arrange the staff-appreciation dinner."

Ellie drops the fork that she was about to use, and her

face turns excited. "Oh yeah… with Knox Blisswood, right?"

"Unfortunately."

Her hands slam down on the table. "Are you kidding me? Your eyes are about to be treated to a fine male specimen for hours."

"Aren't you married?" I remind her, and I'm slightly entertained by her fervor for me.

She chuckles softly. "Oh, I am. But nobody in this town can deny how we all secretly hope that those Blisswood looks come from the Bluetop water and not genetics… Sadly we are inclined to believe it's hereditary."

"We?"

"Yes. Every woman in a ten-mile radius," she confidently declares before popping a bite of pancake into her mouth.

Geez, everyone seems to be under the Blisswood spell. Everyone except me.

"Well, just a shame his personality doesn't match his exterior."

Ellie raises a brow at me. "What do you mean? I mean, yes, out of all the brothers, he is a bit of a rebel and has this kind of edgy vibe happening. But in the end, they are all kind people. In fact, I'm positive he even opened the door for dear old Ms. Woods the other day at school."

"Are we talking about the same person? I'm sure he wakes up every morning wondering which methods he should use to piss someone off that day." I now aggressively try to cut my food with the side of my fork from the pure memory of Knox shaking my pretzels or walking toward my car with his steely look and then the audacity to throw a Mr. Darcy reference into conversation. What fucking nerve.

"Are you okay? Your dessert is looking a little destroyed."

My eyes dart down to the cake now in pieces across my dish. "Completely okay. Why wouldn't I be? Anyway, we're partnered together, so lucky me." I flash my eyes before I grab a piece of cake with my fingers.

"The staff-appreciation dinner is a nice thought. I mean, it's basically the parents paying for us to have a good night. Their way of thanking us for keeping their unruly teenagers in good hands from the hours of 7:50 in the morning to 2:20 in the afternoon, plus extra curriculars. And every year it always ends up at Olive Owl because they basically contribute a lot, so we don't need a big budget," she explains, and I do appreciate the gesture.

"I will keep that in mind when I'm dealing with Satan," I promise.

Ellie goes quiet as she studies me for a few seconds, before she bursts out with a very wide grin then folds her arms and leans back in the booth. "Is Maddie Roads under his spell?"

"You mean a hexed curse brought on by his every breath? Sure. He makes me a wretched person who I don't quite recognize." That's the truth. I do a lot of things in front of that man that I would never do under normal circumstances. Swearing, scowling, challenging, and it gives me energy, which is just crazy.

Knox Blisswood makes me miserable.

But it makes me curious what he will do next.

I'm just not going to admit it out loud.

"You know," she begins by waving a pointed finger at me. "That's a classic recipe for, well… you know… you read that kind of stuff."

I firmly shake my head no.

"We'll see."

"No, we won't. He's a parent of my student, well, sort of. I mean, I'm not sure how to describe it, but it doesn't seem ethical. Besides, I have zero interest. Nada. I do, however, have a strong desire to speed through this whole planning thing with him."

Ellie pushes her plate to the middle of the table. "It's really hate at first sight with him, huh?"

"It is. A first for me too, as normally I'm not quick to judge. Anyhow, I should probably head over there. His majesty mustn't be kept waiting or I'm sure I won't hear the end of it." I grab my wallet from my purse to pull out some money for the bill.

"Send me an SOS if you get desperate, but trust me, you will love it at Olive Owl, and you probably won't want to leave," Ellie mentions as she grabs her own wallet.

"Maybe," I faintly agree, but my skepticism remains strong.

After paying the bill and wishing one another luck on our Sunday-afternoon activities—homework marking for Ellie and demon slaying for myself—we say goodbye. When I get in my car, I have an urge to phone my aunt and uncle. It doesn't take long for my aunt to answer.

"Good morning, Madison," Aunt Carol quickly answers, and as usual, she is in good spirits.

"Hi, Auntie, wanted to check in. How was church today?"

Seeing that my call is set up on my Bluetooth correctly, I begin to drive away from the parking lot in the direction of out of town.

"Wonderful, dear, the choir group is really improving. Your uncle stayed home as he was a little tired," she says, and that isn't news. Uncle Joe should have retired two years ago, but both he and my aunt continue to farm wheat.

"Hopefully this afternoon he can rest. I think the Bears have a pre-season game on."

"Yes, they do, so I will bake some cookies while he watches that. Everything okay, dear? How is the start of the school year?"

I turn right at the stop sign. "Exciting. I'm the new teacher, so all the students wonder about me and try to make good first impressions. Had parent-teacher meetings, and now I'm helping the booster club with a few things. Actually, I need to head to a winery this afternoon to plan a staff dinner. Crazy, huh? Staff dinners at wineries. Not your average small-town high school, that's for sure."

"That sounds absolutely fun." I admire how she is always positive. The mere mention of a winery and I want to punch something. How can it not feel the same for her? I shake out the memory of misfortunes from my head. She mentioned fun, after all, so I should remain optimistic, like she is.

"Maybe. Except this one parent—well, he isn't a parent, a brother of one of my students, really, is just…" I hear the agony in my tone and also recognize that it isn't sincere. "Have you ever met someone who makes you feel like a completely different person that you've never experienced before? Not necessarily in a good way. I mean the kind of way that makes me wonder if I should be going to confessional on Wednesday?"

My aunt begins to laugh really hard. "Oh my! Well, considering we're not Catholic, then yes, something sounds off. But that's life, we are always evolving. Sometimes we need those people in our life to push us."

"Anyway, I just need to suck it up. Plus, I'm sure once I

start handing out homework every day then my life will become occupied with grading."

I see the sign for Olive Owl up ahead and I feel a rush of blood flow through my body, and my heart does something odd too.

"I'm so proud of you, dear, graduating and teaching. I tell everyone about you. When do you think you will visit?" she asks, and it's a question that I knew was coming. I'm closer in most ways to my aunt and uncle than my own parents.

"Probably not until Thanksgiving, as it's Homecoming and Halloween, plus college deadlines. Until November, life is a zoo." I need to make a whole weekend out of visiting my aunt and uncle, so as much as I have some free time, it's not enough to go visit.

"I understand, and we will love to have you here at Thanksgiving."

"I know. Okay, I need to hang up now, as I'm at my destination. I'll call you later in the week, okay?"

"Sounds good, honey. Have fun!"

"Bye."

Pulling into Olive Owl, I lean over my steering wheel to really get a look. Undeniably, it's luscious green grounds, there's a brown horse that looks well taken care of grazing by a fence, a stone path leading to the immaculate big house that must be the inn—a sort of modern farmhouse look. When I look straight ahead, I see a big barn with a wide sliding door, open to show barrels of wine and oil.

Then my eyes land on a place to park, with my demise awaiting.

Knox stands before me with his foot on the wood log breaker at the end of the parking spot. He indicates with his arm that the spot is for me, and that smug delicious smirk seems permanent on his face and—gah—he's wearing jeans and a white tank so well.

This is misery.

And misery loves company, so he comes to my car door as I turn the engine off. He is going to open the door for me. What a jerk.

Taking a deep calming breath, I prepare to be greeted by a man who has the power to piss me off purely by thought.

"Good afternoon, shortcake." He offers me his hand as he smiles.

Rebuffing his efforts, I don't take it and slide out of my seat, pushing him to the side in the process. "Knox."

I stalk forward as he closes my door and follows. "Why, you seem to be in a terrific mood," he says, sarcastic.

I turn to him, and he pauses, as he must see the seriousness on my face as I plant my hands on my hips.

"Let me be clear, Knox. The moment I laid eyes on you, I think I hated you. You think you are some gift on this earth that women adore, but nope. I'm beginning to wonder if you were put on this earth to piss me off. It's such an overpowering feeling, and congratulations, because you are the only person in this universe to have this effect."

My words seem to energize him as he cocks his head to the side. "So, I *do* have an effect on you."

I growl out some indescribable sound, which makes me wonder if this man has me speaking in tongues, while my entire body feels like it's on fire... the fucking good kind that makes me want to do things, like mount his body, to prove a point.

"Can we just get through this afternoon on a unilateral truce?" I suggest.

"Absolutely, shortcake, I put my best foot forward today. Only for you." He winks at me before walking past me.

"We'll see."

While I follow him, he seems to ignore me for the next two minutes as he leads me around the inn to the back stone patio and a garden which is beautifully done, with an area for an outside fire surrounded by rocking chairs. I know they have weddings here, and this is a stunning spot. Yet, it isn't our destination.

Through some tall green plants and a path, he leads me down to a small pond, and next to the pond is a giant willow tree with a wooden swing. But that's only the backdrop.

Because he has a table that is magnificently set and is overloaded with food and wine, plus mason jars filled with a few flowers.

"Here we are," he proudly announces as he turns to me, and the look on his face is indescribable.

"What is this?" I'm slightly lost, as this whole setting looks like the image of a perfect...

The faintest of grins cracks on the corner of his mouth.

Oh no, don't say it. Please don't say it.

"Our *date* for planning, of course." He steps forward, causing our air to merge together.

Damn it, he has a trick up his sleeve.

6

KNOX

Her face is priceless, which is what I was after.

I notice her breath hitch as I move closer to her, enough for me to get a whiff of her flowery shampoo scent and something sweet which I can't quite pinpoint.

"You see, I woke up with the thought of how I could piss you off the most, since it seems you feel that's my life mission, and to be honest, I'm beginning to think that today it may be true." I begin to circle around her, which causes her body to stiffen, but her eyes stayed glued to me as she seems curious what I will do. Bringing a finger to my chin, I pretend to think. "What could I do that would really aggravate Madison to no end, I thought to myself. Then it dawned on me that you must have lost a lot of sleep last night knowing you would be seeing me. And then, when you finally did sleep, I'm sure I was in your dreams too. So what could I do to really get under your skin?"

"Why yes, yes, you were absolutely in my *nightmares* last night, and trust me, when I laid awake at night, it was because I was trying to fathom how the hell to survive the next few weeks with you," she corrects me with a snipe.

I smile at her feistiness that I seem to bring out in her. "I know anything that resembles a date really gets you in a frenzy, which is exactly what I want. So it looks like today is a win for me," I tell her as I attempt to brush a loose strand of her hair behind her ear, to which she replies by swatting my fingers away.

She marches forward and for show moves the chair out. "Do your worst, Knox. I promise you that my opinion of you won't change."

"Wow, so obedient today, is it a full moon?" I follow her to the table.

We both get comfortable in our seats and enter a stare-off, it seems.

"Wine?" I offer.

"No."

"Cheese and crackers?"

"No, I just ate."

"Water?"

"Only if you didn't taint it with who knows whatever punch you have the people around here drinking."

Now I sigh because this woman doesn't relent. She has a vendetta, and I'm not quite sure why. I haven't done anything to her, other than exist. This conversation feels like pulling teeth out, yet somehow, I still want to stay invested in this afternoon.

Ignoring her for a second, I pour myself a glass of red wine, as I need it.

"Chocolate-covered pretzel?" I tilt my head in the direction of the bowl that is my secret weapon.

Her eyes draw a line from me to the carbs. She seems

skeptical and pleasantly surprised. "Half a point for effort… maybe."

She slowly drags the bowl in her direction, before grabbing a piece.

Leaning back in my chair, I decide we should talk business for a minute to knock that out of the way. "Okay, so this staff-appreciation dinner. Same thing every year. Mini wine tasting upon arrival, with cheeses, then a light three-course dinner with vegetarian or beef option, then dessert of chocolate mousse. Start time 4pm and aim to finish by 10pm. Helen will provide a little basket with small samples of jam and olive oil as a parting gift. Sound good?"

Maddie's eyebrows knit together, as I just basically answered any questions she may have had. "We don't need to go over menus?"

"You heard me, right? Vegetarian or beef."

"The wine?"

I scoff a laugh. "You hate it, remember? It's already sorted which ones."

"*So*… basically it's already planned?"

"You really don't listen. It never changes. Every year the same."

Her tongue circles her mouth as she looks off into the distance for a second before refocusing her attention on me. "Why am I here then?"

"Oh, that's purely for my own kicks. This is fun, isn't it?" I casually say before drinking from my wine glass.

"Un-fucking-believable." She is now ready to murder me.

"You know, you swear like a sailor, considering you are supposed to be a respectable English teacher."

She rubs the sides of her head with her fingers. "Only

around you am I like this. So, congrats for bringing out the worst in me."

"That does make me kind of proud," I reply.

"I'm out of here."

She stands, and immediately, I follow suit so we are on the same level.

"Don't you want a tour? You're here anyway."

"No. No, I don't. I have no interest in a winery that for some reason everyone believes is the best thing to happen this side of the Mississippi, when in reality you probably destroyed some small farm nearby in the process so you can produce some organic liquid. Or this whole most-romantic-place label has to be bullshit and just seems like you probably slept with whoever the hell wrote that blog that made this place famous. So no, I really don't want to stay, Knox. This place is everything that just makes me want to…"

Now I'm pissed off, and even with the fury building inside of me, I picked up on a strong undertone of something bothering her that has nothing to do with me.

"You know what, Madison? I have no clue what is inside of your cold heart. But from day one, you have only thought the worst of me, and you don't even know me. And everything you just said is complete bullshit. So how about you get off your high horse and actually learn some facts."

Both of our eyes are blazing with anger.

"Enlighten me," she challenges and crosses her arms like a fucking toddler.

This woman. Unmanageable.

"Firstly, we're not an organic farm because it's fucking hard to follow every rule to get that status, especially with all the neighboring farms using fertilizer and pesticides. The neighboring farms that we have done nothing to. They happily grow their corn, and we grow our grapes and olives. In fact, the farmers' market? The only thing that remotely resembles someone pissed off is the ladies who battle over being labeled as best jam and pies. Want to talk about ruthless? Those women can cut through you with a stare. So how about you erase whatever notion you may have fucking had about Olive Owl." I collapse in my chair as soon as I finish my rant.

Her upper lip twitches as if she wants to smile. "Cutthroat jams and pies, huh?"

"Yeah, Helen is going to take Sally-Anne down this year with her lemon meringue."

A silence comes over us, and Madison slowly sits back down.

"I take it you didn't sleep with the blogger?"

I look up at her and scoff. "Really?" I doubt her. "Why would you care? Or is it because you're interested in my talents?"

She ruefully shakes her head and at last a wry smile forms on her lips. Our eyes connect for a moment and then she grabs the bottle of wine and pours herself a very small glass.

"I'm sorry... I was a little fired up," she softly attempts to apologize.

"No shit."

"I'm a little sensitive around wineries."

"Oh yeah? I hadn't noticed," I sarcastically respond.

"There was one that started near my aunt and uncle's place and basically destroyed their land in the process because whatever they used for their plants got into the air and then affected my aunt and uncle's wheat. They almost had to start over."

Ah, that is a piece of the puzzle.

"That's why you're not a fan of Olive Owl? You associate all wineries as evil?"

She nods in agreement. "I perhaps jumped to conclusions, and I'm... sorry." Madison quickly sips from her wine as if her sentence was ripping off a band-aid.

"Wow... is your heart defrosting from that apology?"

Her lips quirk out as she sets her glass down.

I attempt to sympathize. "It sucks, I'm sure. I maybe understand where you're coming from. I've heard many stories of people's crops just going to dust thanks to a new farmer. I'm sorry it happened to them." I mean it sincerely too.

Madison seems to pick up on this. "Thanks... Anyways." She nervously plays with the stem of the wine glass. "It's alright wine."

"Alright?" I throw a grape into my mouth.

"It's... good," she admits and tries to hide that beautiful smile that is natural to her.

I don't respond, only get comfortable in my chair and watch her eyes wander around the scene and table.

"You're very protective of Olive Owl," she comments as she grabs another pretzel.

"Of course I am. It's my family's, and it's grown so much since I was a kid."

Her tongue darts out to the corner of her mouth and my eyes become fixated, and I think I may be jealous of her tongue.

"You never wanted to leave Bluetop?"

"Nah, I have everything I want here. Unlike my brothers, I kind of want to stay living on this plot until they need to bury me."

Her head gently tilts to the side, and after a moment, she slides out of her chair. At first, panic hits me that she's leaving, but then I feel relief when she walks to the swing that is hanging from the tree.

"I love these. My aunt and uncle made one for me at their farm. It was the highlight of all my summers." She fondly looks at the wood seat hanging by ropes that she touches between her fingers.

Standing, I walk to the other side of the swing. "Is that where you learned to use a tractor?"

Her eyes gaze up at me, and they are sparkly with the sun and her appreciation that I didn't forget. "You remembered?"

"It was random thing to mention, so yeah, it stuck with me. Go on." I indicate for her to sit on the swing.

She laughs at my suggestion. "I don't think—I mean, isn't this for kids or something?"

"I'm sure Rosie, my niece, won't mind. She's the reason we have it. When we were kids, we had a tire swing, but then got rid of it. When Grayson returned to town, he quickly became crazy about Rosie, and the tree house at the other end of the property is in the works for next summer."

"Ah yes, the brother that I was supposed to meet with. The one that probably wouldn't come up with schemes to get me here." Her eyes go wide before she sits on the swing.

"Trust me, you'll have more fun with me," I promise. I look down at her as she begins to sway back and forth using her foot.

She laughs at my thought. "You are trouble, Knox, that's what you are."

"You're insufferable, but here I am."

"Insufferable and proud." She walks back to propel herself on the swing, causing me to step back.

My hand weaves through my hair as I watch her and

the way her blonde locks flow in the slight breeze. Admittedly, she looks like she belongs here under this tree.

I want to know more about her, I'm far too curious.

"You mentioned your aunt and uncle a few times. You must be close with them."

She glances over her shoulder back at me as she swings forward. "Wow, he connects dots and observes."

Now I'm the one who shakes my head ruefully.

"Yes, I'm close with them. I used to spend almost all my summers and school breaks with them."

"Why is that?" I pry as I scratch my chin.

She abruptly stops the swing then stands, leaving the ropes to move in the wake of her departure.

"This tour you were talking about, do I get the VIP version or the version where you trap me in some dungeon?" She's changing the topic, but I let it go because she is also agreeing to stay.

"Depends if rope-tying actually excites you." I wiggle my brows at her before walking past her.

I don't need to look back to know she is trying to hide a grin.

We walk for the next twenty minutes. I show her the grapes and olives, and to my surprise, she has a few question in relation to agriculture. By the time I show her the barrels of wine, I'm beginning to feel that I have cleared all negative thoughts she may have had about Olive Owl.

Her smile has brightened by the time we reach the chickens and Cosmo, my sister's horse.

"He's beautiful. Do you ride him?" she asks as she lets the horse sniff her hand, as his head is over the fence.

"Nah, I leave that to Lucy. You? Ride horses?"

"I did, but it's been a while. I'm surprised you don't

have a dog. This is the kind of place that needs a dog." She looks at me as she pets Cosmo's brown fur.

My hand rubs the back of my neck. "We had a Labrador as a kid. A good guy, lived until he was 14. You?"

Her lips quirk out. "I wish. My parents were adamant, no dogs in the house. Now I live in an apartment, so it wouldn't be fair to a dog. I want a giant dog. So, what do you do in your spare time, Knox?"

Leaning against the fence, I tell her, "I find ways to get into your head, of course. How am I doing?"

"You may need to try harder." She steps away, and suddenly she is leading the way while I follow, my eyes stuck on her body that moves gracefully in a swayed walk.

When we reach the main house, I run a few steps in front of her to open the door. "See? Gentleman."

"Questionable." She walks past me, and I notice her eyes scan the area that has a bar and dining area. It's empty now, as we have no guests this evening or tastings.

"Normally, we have the fireplace on, but it's a little too hot out for that. The guests have breakfast in the small dining room if they spend the night."

Her head sharply turns to my direction. "I needed to know that detail?" She raises a brow.

I chuckle under my breath, liking that her mind went there. "*Those* guests get breakfast in my bed."

She hums a sound. "I'm sure they do."

Walking farther into the room, she heads to the window overlooking the back and where we had our picnic earlier. "It is a beautiful place."

"And?"

"I can... understand why people get a little mystified over it."

My hands find my jeans pockets as I take in the way

she looks at everything. Not just looks but appreciates. I'm totally screwed because she understands things about Olive Owl that most do not, she's hot as hell, and she fucking dislikes me which is only fuel.

"Do you want to go back to the picnic?" I ask, secretly hopeful.

"Oh." I seem to catch her off guard and she nibbles her bottom lip. "Not sure we have much to talk about now that everything is already arranged and you've shown me the Blisswood empire."

"Eggs?" I throw in another try to get her to stay. "I mean, do you want to take some eggs for home?"

"You just want me to look at your cock, don't you?" She has a sultry look on her face, and I think my dick just woke, ready for action.

The surprise on my face from her bold statement causes her to laugh, then clarify. "The rooster? I mean *that* cock." She pats my shoulder in comfort for the fact that she just sent my body into shock. Then she walks in the direction of the exit.

I blow out a breath between my pursed lips to try and calm my guy down, then yet again today follow the woman who somehow walks around as if she owns this place.

But sadly, we don't get any cock action, as she clicks the fob of her car which is the indication that she is leaving.

"Thanks for luring me out here."

"I don't think presenting facts and proving how wrong you were is luring," I correct her as I open the car door for her.

"I was wrong about Olive Owl, Knox. Not you," she counters as she slides into her seat.

My face is puzzled, and inside I'm slightly wounded

that she still has me on a hit list. "Does that mean I'm still in your bad book?"

"You make feel completely agitated."

"There are ways to work that out," I remind her, and it causes her to roll her eyes.

"See, already I want to swipe that smug look off your face." She puts the fob in the ignition and the engine turns on.

"Swipe right?"

She can't hide the smile that erupts on her face.

Leaning down so we are on the same eye level, I'm honest about my plan. "You see, Madison, I think you very much enjoy my antics, which is why you are escaping now instead of partaking in the alternative."

"Alternative?"

I lick my lips and move into her space which causes her to adjust in her seat, possibly because she needs to cross her legs from the feeling that my mere presence gives her. "The one where we can enjoy a glass of wine and find something to argue about until we decide that being around one another is much better when we keep you quiet."

I reach out one finger to touch her soft lips that feel like heaven.

She's left speechless for a few moments until she breaks our contact by quickly grabbing her seatbelt. But again, I stop her by taking the band of the seatbelt from her then reaching over her to ensure our bodies brush, and her body trembles as I buckle her in. My own mouth trails an invisible line an inch or two from along the outline of her cheek and across her mouth. So close, but not enough to touch.

"Until next time, shortcake," I say as I move back and out of the car.

She bites her bottom lip, and as her entire body sinks into the seat, she gathers herself.

"Careful, Knox. I put teenagers in detention on a daily basis; I have no qualms doing my worst to you," she warns.

"Be my guest. Detention with you sounds like a dream."

I close her car door, but it doesn't block the sound of her grumble.

The crazy part is, even though I don't let it show, I feel the absolute same.

She's infuriating, and now I need a cold shower.

Next time, I won't be so gentlemanly. No, I will absolutely blow her mind instead.

7

MADISON

I stare at the seventeen-year-old in front of me who is sitting at his desk and typing away on his cell phone, waiting for him to get a clue.

"Phone. Desk. Now. End of day you can collect it," I instruct with my stern teacher voice and tilt my head in the direction of the front of the class.

Braden let's out a disgruntled sound then obeys.

My attention moves to the rest of the class as I walk between the rows. "I want a five-page essay by the end of the week on the book that you chose from the list of options. Remember to keep those essays in a good structure with an intro paragraph, three paragraphs of points, and a conclusion. I'm not so concerned about grammar— although you should watch that. I'm going to grade on content and the way you insert your opinions supported by plot points. Okay, that's it for today."

The movement of notebooks and pens informs me they were actually listening and jotting down my assignment just before the bell rings to dismiss them. Returning to my desk, I sit and take in the sound of students leaving the room. I now have a free period to gather my thoughts and grab a snack.

However, not even a minute in and I hear a soft knock on my door. Glancing up, I see a man who I've seen around here once or twice. My mind does a quick run-through of names and then I realize that it's Grayson Blisswood. The man that I should have had the parent-teacher meeting with.

"Sorry to interrupt." It's true. That Blisswood charm is hereditary, based purely on a smile, and they all wear a pair of jeans to perfection.

"It's okay. What can I do for you, Mr. Blisswood?" I reply with a soft look.

He walks farther into my room and perches against a desk in the front row. "Please, it's Grayson, and I was here, as I am helping Coach Dingle with the football team later, and thought I would come check in. I hear you got stuck with my brother for booster-club duty."

I search his facial expression for a clue as to what this conversation could possibly be about. So, I play it cool. "I did. Is there a last-minute change? Are you taking his place again?" I may be hopeful.

Being stuck with a married man who has no interest in any other soul is a safe option. Being stuck with Knox who makes every fiber of my body heat up is not safe at all—in fact, it's dangerous.

He waves off that notion. "Nah, he's already in too deep, plus Lucy would kill me if I were around here even more than I already am. I heard you both may have started on the wrong foot. I can only imagine what he must have done. He can be difficult sometimes. I just wanted to check that my brother has been on good behavior? I mean, he isn't causing you any trouble?"

"Good behavior?" I gulp. He most certainly is not on

good behavior. He should be sent to the doghouse, especially after his seatbelt trick the other week.

"Yeah, not giving you a hard time with any of the planning stuff? Why, has he done something else?" he innocently asks.

I scratch the back of my neck, as I feel suddenly uncomfortable, quite possibly because the mere thought of Knox Blisswood sends me to unknown depths. "Everything is dandy."

Dandy? What the hell?

Grayson finds my answer humorous, I can tell. He scratches his chin as he seems to be thinking over something. "Great. Well, I also wanted to thank you for sending me the e-mail with all the information. Brooke and I will make sure that Lucy is on top of everything, but she doesn't really need us. She's got this. At dinner last night, she mentioned something about extracurricular stuff?"

I rest my folded hands on my desk, causing me to feel very official. "Right, I would like her to help with the English-as-a-second-language group. I have some freshmen who could use help with reading. I think it would be a wonderful addition to her applications, but only if it isn't too much for her. Putting too much on her plate isn't a good idea either."

He quirks his lips out as he thinks about it. "Sounds good. She seemed on board last night too. Hey, by any chance are you a chocolate-chip-cookie fan?"

My brows furrow, as he took a sharp turn in our conversation direction. "Um, I guess... why?"

"Perfect. Brooke makes the best cookies around." He claps his hands together once. "Would you be up for dinner? I mean, Lucy would love it, Brooke too. Hell, the whole family. It's the least we could do to get to know Lucy's new favorite teacher." His peppy tone concerns me.

My teacher radar that I quickly developed picks up on a warning sign.

I tightly smile and try to swallow the entertainment of this all. "Grayson, it's okay. You don't need to bribe me to write a positive recommendation for Lucy for her applications. Besides, the other parents already sent me caramel popcorn, invited me to Sunday dinner, or even volunteered to change the oil in my car for free. So I'm kind of bribed out." I click the inside of my cheek and offer a grin.

He frowns at my answer before his own grin cracks out. "Ah, senior year; not just crazy for the students."

I chuckle at his observation. "No, not at all."

"Well, just let me know if you change your mind. Wine? Eggs? We have olive oil—"

I cut him off by raising my hand to motion for him to stop. "Really, I'm stocked up. By the way, Olive Owl is really beautiful, and the wine isn't half bad. It was like a setting from *The Secret Garden*, that table near the old wooden swing and pond."

A peculiar look comes over Grayson as lines form on his forehead. "You just, uh, had a tour or did my brother actually offer you refreshments sans rat poison?"

I snicker at the thought because it was a whole buffet that he offered. "Oh, don't worry, he was low on poison that day, so I'm still alive, and he had every option of refreshments splayed out on the table." *Himself included.*

"Really? For planning the staff dinner?" The pitch of his voice suddenly concerns me, and I realize I just explained the other weekend far too simply.

"Mmhmm." I gulp.

"The staff dinner that is the same thing every year?" His eyes grow big.

Pretending to grab a paper from the side, I answer honestly and reluctantly. "I came to realize that... *after* I arrived."

Grayson abruptly stands and seems satisfied with the information that I just accidentally shared. "Sounds like Knox has everything under control then." He walks to the door of my classroom then pauses and turns to look at me once more. "You know Knox hates having picnics under the willow tree."

I look at him blankly. "And?"

"Reminds him of our mother." He watches me as I listen and I realize it's a sentimental fact, and my face must show it. His hand knocks the inner door pane. "I guess he was just presenting options for the staff dinner, right?" He winks at me before leaving.

My face turns a shade of red discovering that I'm the exception, and internally, a chip on my Knox Blisswood wall is broken off.

————

My FEET HIT the gravel path of the trail. Power-walking to my heart's content doesn't seem to be helping to clear my thoughts. The trees of the forest around me are beginning to turn color, and my guess is this is probably the last weekend of the year where we will have warm temps. Fall is officially here.

Considering it is just past eight on a Saturday morning, it isn't that busy. My arms swing as I walk, wearing my favorite pants that fit me like a glove, and I have a new loose gray tank top over a hot-pink sports bra. I find the cuter I feel when I work out, the better I move.

It should be an easy-going weekend, except for the fact I have about four hours of grading papers to do, of which probably fifty percent are students clearly having watched the movie instead of reading the actual book that they chose.

I take some yogi breaths as I take in my surroundings; morning sun, sounds of chirping birds, and the occasional *good morning* from someone passing by on their bike or run.

I'm busy looking ahead on the gravel when I hear someone call me. Ugh, just his voice rattles me to my core.

"Shortcake, working out some tension?" Knox runs a few steps in front of me before jogging backward.

His presence causes me to pick up my pace. "Knox." I do my best to avoid his gaze, but I already see he has on running shorts and a tight gray tee, with sweat droplets falling around the curves of his face.

"Well, good morning to you too."

I stop in my walk to look up, and my fists form at my sides next to my hips. "Surprised you're here this morning. Did your Friday-night hookup leave before dawn when she realized what a mistake it must have been?"

"Wow. That's a low blow. Would you believe me if I said I was happily content reading Pasternak last night alone in my room?"

My head perks up from his reference. "Right, what was the title of the book then?" Surely, he is lucky with his guess.

He steps closer to me to invade my air, and I already feel his confidence. "*Doctor Zhivago*. I'm debating if it's better than the movie."

"Fortunate guess." I brush past him because my body can't handle him so close.

"How was your thrilling evening?"

"Fine." I continue my walking journey, but I feel him moving next to me.

"You know you seem a little wound up. Are you sure your method of exercise is working? You may need to find other outlets of stress release," he suggests as he looks forward, and I don't need to side-eye to know he has a smirk plastered on his face.

Rolling my eyes, I play along. "Let me guess, you have an idea and can demonstrate."

"Nah, something tells me you don't need a demonstration, you know exactly how to do it. By the way, I feel like we never addressed the elephant in the room. Why isn't there a Mr. Uptight in the picture?"

Aggravation floods me and I stop to turn to him. "Not that it's any of your business but I had a boyfriend until six months ago. Sometimes it just doesn't work out, and nor did I want to move to Seattle where he got a job. What's your excuse, Knox? Aren't you some holier-than-thou Blisswood that every woman falls for? Yet here you are stalking me bright and early."

He stands taller and steps closer to me. "Maddie, I don't want every woman. So kill me for being choosey."

Puffing out a breath, I feel like we are always in a circle in our conversations. "Anyway, I should head back to my car."

"Me too, I need to get to the farmers' market, as we have a stall."

It causes a natural smile to spread on my face. "I love farmers' markets. My aunt and uncle always go. You can get the best lettuce there."

"And men, if that's what you're after."

My eyes flick up to meet his piercing gaze that makes a flutter float inside of me. "Cute." I begin to walk but I notice he doesn't follow, which causes me to stop in curiosity because surely he wants to harass me longer. "What?"

He looks at me, clearly amused, as he scratches the scruff on his face that I want to feel scratching against my skin. "The parking lot is the other way."

"No, it's not. It's this way." I point in the direction that I was heading.

"No, Maddie, it's that way." He points in the opposite direction.

Looking around, I realize that I actually have no clue where I am, as the trees all look the same after a while.

But I don't want him to be right. "I'm positive it's this way."

"You're never agreeable, are you?"

My chest sticks out as I reach overhead to tighten my ponytail. "With you? No, no, I'm not."

"Want to go your way to find out if I'm right? You may need to run, as it's an extra half-mile to circle back to the parking lot. I can handle it, but I'm not sure your stubborn tendencies can."

"Ugh." My hand shoves him to the side so I can walk past him. "Or you go your way and I go my way, then I will see you some other time."

"Not doing that. If you get lost and eaten alive, who will I have to aggravate me at the staff-appreciation dinner next week?" He begins to follow me.

"I'm not going to be eaten alive. Coyotes don't come out during this time of day, and I know what poison ivy looks like." I begin my fast walking with a secret hope he doesn't give in; I want him to follow me.

He does. Thankfully.

"Okay, lead the way. Shall we run? Or are you out of shape since you spend more time training your hand?"

"You are so fucking vulgar." I continue my quest forward.

He snickers at me as he walks next to me. "Says the teacher who literally put the f-bomb and vulgar in the same sentence. Plus, I'm not particularly feeling like a gentleman today. You have this uncanny knack for giving me a headache, yet I can't seem to stay away."

"Feeling is mutual."

"Great. Shall we discuss world peace or is this where you tell me you have a thing for the wilderness and a hot guy who pins you against a tree?" he says in a neutral tone.

"Depends if he ties me to the tree or not," I retort then glance to my side to see his reaction which is a sexy kind of surprised.

"Let me guess, you'll help tighten the knot?"

I cluck my tongue and pick up my pace.

"There is a spot, in case you're interested, down by a small cave with Native American writing on the wall."

Scoffing a sound, I refute. "No, thank you. Don't need to go where you probably lost your v-card."

"Oh, that wasn't here."

For some reason, I'm too invested in this conversation. "Humor me. Who was the lucky victim?"

"Sophie Plums, back of my car, sophomore year of high school."

I choke on my own breath and stop in my tracks. "The mom who gave you fuck-me eyes at the booster club meeting?"

"You noticed that too? I thought it was wildly inappropriate." He plays innocent but the grin doesn't fade. "And yeah, we were together for two months. That was before she went on to have an affair with a married man in college then became trophy wife number two and is now a stepmom to a teenage kid."

My head lolls to the side. "Huh, was wondering about that set-up."

"You?"

"Freshman year of college, dorm room. Nothing too exciting. We broke up four months later," I admit, but I'm okay with it too. It was a guy I was dating for a little bit, he was patient, and it was... well, nothing mind-blowing.

Shaking my head, I realize what we are talking about on a Saturday morning before my first coffee of the day. Yet my mouth spits out the most ridiculous sentence of the week. "So... Sophie Plums." It would be simple enough, except my words are drenched in some bizarre jealousy.

"You're kind of cute in a snarling-not-going-to-show-you're-affected kind of way."

"I'm not affected," I reply blankly and look at my watch to see my heartrate is elevated, and I feel an urge to flee. "Maybe we should run."

My feet are already moving before my mind catches up that I don't run. Never. Ever. My legs are incapable of moving faster than a power walk. Yet now I'm sprinting.

Knox runs too, and suddenly it feels like a competition —who can escape the other first.

Obviously, he has an advantage due to his height and the fact the man is built like a Greek god. Still, I torture myself and push myself harder. In response, he goes faster, causing me to try more.

It's a brutal few minutes, and when the parking lot

finally appears in the distance, I'm surprised I'm still alive, and the cool-down walk the last few hundred feet is paradise.

I'm covered in sweat, and so is Knox who's watching me almost with concern. "You're going to feel that tomorrow."

My panting breaths don't allow me to answer. Instead, I plant my hands on my thighs and hunch over to catch my breath.

"Shortcake, you good? Or am I going to have to give you CPR soon? My version, of course." He stands there watching me with his arms folded.

"You..." I point a finger and continue to try and normalize my breathing. I give up on giving him a jab back and instead slowly follow him to his car which is conveniently next to my own.

We both hit our car fobs and grab water bottles from the back seats of our vehicles. Knox takes a good drink, then throws it back onto the seat before peeling his shirt up and off to reveal his chiseled chest and abs that are covered in sweat, and my eyes track every droplet.

Now I can't breathe, and it isn't from the run. My mouth parts open and I'm unable to break my stare away.

"Don't drool, shortcake," he reprimands me with smoldering eyes.

He will not have the upper hand, no, I will not let him.

My hands grab the edges of my tank and ceremoniously quickly whip it up and off my body to leave me there in my sports bra and sweaty skin. To be fair, it's one of those bras that could be worn alone. His brows instantly arch as his eyes scan me from head to toe. Clearly he's impressed that I'm not afraid to have a little stand-off with him, clothing optional.

"Stop calling me shortcake, or anything sweet," I demand with a stern look.

His smug look doesn't fade as he steps to me, causing me to back into my car. I'm trapped between him and my door, with no escape. Which I don't mind, as I want to see what he'll do.

He sets his forearms above me against the car, and the smell of our sweat merges as our eyes stay fixed.

The he leans in, and his breath crawls up my neck until his mouth is near the shell of my ear. My internal walls are clenching for survival, and I pray the tingling in my breasts fades.

"That's because I'm quite confident you taste like a fucking dessert. I hate dessert, but there is always an exception."

Slowly he backs away, the back of his finger drawing a line along my cheekbone down to my jaw.

"You know I like you wet everywhere," he comments.

I'm speechless. How does this man have the power to crumble my walls of steel that I thought I had? Why do I want to drown in his attention?

"You'll never know if I'm wet everywhere," I rasp before breaking out of his trap.

I scurry to the driver's side of the car, but I still hear him call out.

"Don't forget that I'll be seeing you at the staff-appreciation dinner next weekend. Don't get too dressed up, I don't need much for my imagination when it comes to you."

I'm totally screwed.

8

KNOX

S traightening a few bottles of olive oil and wine on the stall table, I glance up at my brother Grayson arriving, and he is holding our nephew, Bennett's son, J.J., in one of those baby carrier things.

"Here for duty," Grayson reports before looking down at the kid and cooing.

"Is Bennett in the parking lot doing things to his wife that we don't particularly want to imagine?"

"Probably," he responds before grabbing a bottle from the box to set on the table.

I give him a knowing grin. "Or is it baby duty to try and persuade your wife to expand the fam?"

"Bingo." Grayson has no problem admitting his tactic.

The farmers' market is only once a month and every season except winter, because nobody wants to be outside in Illinois winter, well, except to get Christmas trees, but people just come straight to our farm to collect those.

Bluetop Market is a day everyone marks on their calendars and plans around accordingly. It's the day to size up the local produce, catch up on gossip, and see who is battling it out for best baked goods and jams.

"So, little brother... how is it going with the booster club?" Grayson has that tone. The I-have-a-theory tone.

"Fine, why?" I move a crate under the clothed table.

Grayson's mouth twitches from a smile threatening to form. "I met Ms. Roads. She mentioned you were very hospitable with planning the staff-appreciation dinner."

"Hospitable? Me? She would never say that."

"Okay, she didn't. Actually, she seemed kind of annoyed that you got her to Olive Owl under false pretenses, but anyway, she also mentioned the beautiful picnic... under the tree, next to the swing..."

I blow out a breath. I know that he probably wants to make a big deal out of the fact that I don't really chill under that tree. That used to be the spot that my mom would always make us sit for a picnic of fresh cookies or lemonade. Not even Rosie, my niece, can get me to sit there for her tea parties.

My mom passed when Lucy was born, and that was seventeen years ago. I dealt with it, just like I dealt with my dad's recent death; I moved on. I don't dwell, but there are the little things, reminders, that somehow catch me off guard, or things that I avoid because they might trigger a memory.

Yet that day I felt a need to sit under that tree with a table of food for a woman who thinks I'm the devil. Because it all seemed... fitting.

"And? She'd never tried our wine, so I let her try the wine." I move us along, and just as Grayson is opening his mouth to add his two cents, Bennett and Kelsey arrive looking like two humans who just did everything you shouldn't do in a public parking lot.

We look at them peculiarly.

"Here is your kid back," Grayson says as he gently hands J.J. back to Bennett as Brooke and Rosie arrive too.

"What's the game plan, kids?" I ask as I straighten yet another bottle of wine on the table.

"J is staying with us, he is a marketing genius." Bennett pinches his son's chubby cheek, and I agree with his theory, as women of all ages hang around us when they see the baby, then feel compelled to buy our goods.

Kelsey helps strap the baby to Bennett. "I'm completely on board with you using our son. Okay, ladies' afternoon today. Where is Lucy? She said she would meet us here."

"I'll text her… or not," Brooke mentions as she tips her head up in the direction behind them.

Everyone seems to focus on my sister marching toward us. I don't pay much attention until she speaks.

"You," she seethes out and points to me.

Oh man, she is in one of her moods again. "Uh-oh, what did I do?" I'm not too concerned, so I focus on drinking from my water bottle.

"You slept with my new English teacher!" she yells.

Okay, didn't see that coming.

Everyone's faces drop and they focus all their attention on me.

"The one you said was uptight and a pain in your ass?" Grayson asks me, reminding me of our group text a few weeks back.

"You mean her—the one who you said you would choose poison over despite her appeal?" Bennett asks, and yes, I may have said that.

My jaw goes slack, and I can only grin awkwardly. "That's the one," I confirm as I scratch my cheek. "I guess I should explain this…"

"Oh, please do." Bennett crosses his arms and looks on, entertained.

I flash him a fake smile before striding forward to Lucy, grab her arm, and walk her away from the group.

When I let her arm go, her attitude is apparent on her face as we look at one another. "Clue me in, Lucy, what in the world makes you think that I'm sleeping with Madi— Ms. Roads?"

"So you're not going to deny this?" Her entire body is stiff from annoyance.

I blow out some irritation. I would like us not to go in a circle. "Lucy, who the hell I sleep with isn't really your business."

Okay. Not the most diffusing of answers, I admit.

Her face drops and her hands find her waist. "Fuck, Knox."

Holding a hand up, I attempt to calm her. "I'm not." *Yet.* "Explain to me why you arrived hell bent and ready to crucify me?"

Lucy studies me with her scowl not fading. "Kendall said she saw you and Ms. Roads together and you both looked... *cozy*." The disdain in her final word is clear.

Sighing, I pinch the bridge of my nose while I remind myself that as much as Lucy isn't a little kid anymore, her friends haven't matured as quickly. Kendall has been her best friend since kindergarten and enjoys gossip as much as she enjoys cheerleading and football players.

"Right, so if Kendall says it then it must be true?" I don't blink as I let it sink into Lucy how ridiculous her source of facts is. "Tell me, what does Kendall think she saw?"

"You and Ms. Roads in a compromising position at the

parking lot of the forest preserve." Her brow raises as she seems confident that it's a legitimate fact.

I play it cool. "Okay, so what? Two adults having a discussion in a very public parking lot. Not exactly a game changer."

"You weren't shirtless?" she challenges me.

Fuck, the hole I'm digging is getting a little bigger.

"After a long run, yes, I was. What the hell is Kendall doing there in the early morning?"

Lucy awkwardly adjusts her posture as she seems uncomfortable.

I just continue to stare at her and wait for an answer, because she knows that I won't take bullshit. "Ugh, she fell asleep with Braden in his car last night."

I roll my eyes. "Jesus, tell me no more."

"It isn't true?"

"Me and Madison... I mean, Ms. Roads? No, she probably wants to make some witches brew to curse me."

Lucy looks at me, puzzled. "But she is so nice, the sweetest."

"So I've heard." I place my hand on her shoulder and guide her back toward our family.

"Just, please, I know you two are buddied together, but can you just not go there with my teacher?" she innocently requests.

It piques my interest enough. "Lucy, why does it matter?"

"Because... I just... I just want a normal senior year. Is that so crazy? I don't think my brother sleeping with my college advisor is exactly smooth sailing. Plus, I would have to switch classes."

I hear the sincerity in her request. What she really means is after the last few years full of changes when our dad died, Grayson moved back, and Bennett became a father, this is the year she may have a normal school year.

"Sure," I tell her and realize that I can't make a promise.

Probably, I should address that, but for now there is nothing for Lucy to worry about.

"All good?" Grayson checks in as we return to the group.

"False alarm," Lucy informs everyone.

"You will calm the gossip train?" I check with Lucy, and she nods in agreement.

Kelsey and Brooke are quick to huddle around Lucy, and it doesn't take long for them to excuse themselves for their afternoon of whatever women do when they are together.

That leaves me with my brothers who both stare at me, their subtle grins a warning that the next ten minutes may just be an interrogation.

"Really?" Bennett tilts his head to the side. "The teacher?"

"Relax, it's all rumor."

Grayson chuckles under his breath. "For now?"

Rolling my eyes, I move to behind the stall and adjust the small sign listing our prices.

"Wait, can someone fill me in? I thought you strongly dislike the woman. How did we go from that to our teenage sister thinking you are doing wicked things with her teacher?" Bennett looks puzzled.

"Teenagers have wild imaginations, what can I say?" I sigh.

"Except... maybe you don't want it to be a rumor," Grayson mentions.

I slam a bottle of oil down. "Who the hell cares what I

want. You two are busy enough with your wives and offspring, let me be."

"Touchy." Bennett bounces his son as he holds him close to his chest.

"Look." Grayson holds his hands up and looks between us. "Just be… vigilant."

Blowing out a breath, I volunteer to get a round of coffees. "Refreshments anyone?"

"Change of topic, real smooth," Bennett chastises me. "Just don't be an ass, and if you like the woman then fine, we are only saying maybe don't screw this up too badly… for Lucy."

"Says the man who knocked up his fuck-buddy, sure, I'll listen to you." My mundane tone shows my enthusiasm.

"You mean my now wife, yes… yes, you should listen to me," Bennett warns me with a stern look.

Grayson hands a bottle of oil to a customer and quickly speaks over his shoulder back to me. "I'm just going to stand on the sidelines and watch this all unfold. The you-and-Madison thing."

"Doesn't she dislike you?" Bennett reminds me.

"Exactly, so we are not a thing. The woman wants to feed me to vultures, discussion closed."

Grayson smiles at my brother and me. "Except that's exactly the way you like her. A challenging woman is the one you've been waiting for."

Completely true too, which means he isn't wrong.

I only nod in acknowledgment with a tight smile.

———

THE NEXT WEEKEND ROLLS AROUND, and it's the Bluetop High staff-appreciation dinner. Everything is ready to go, from nicely set tables to the wine and food. There is nothing better than seeing the adults who lead our future generation let loose.

Helen shimmies my way as I hold a wine glass in the air to examine if it's clean.

"Knox, everything looks wonderful. Did Ms. Roads help you? Where is she?" Helen searches around the room. "She was supposed to assist you."

If there were actually things for her to do, sure. But this was all handled already, as it is every year, and Madison is a smart cookie, so she texted me earlier today.

Madison: I'm assuming you have everything under control seeing as I had no involvement in the planning. And considering that fact, then I guess I don't need to waste extra minutes of my life with you one-on-one. I'll be on time. Tootles.

I give Helen an overdone smile. "Ms. Roads was a real treat when it came to arranging everything that you had already picked out, gave us a specific list for, and left zero room for imagination. She'll be here soon—"

My head does a double take as I see Madison sway into the inn in slow motion, hair blowing, John Mayer soundtrack playing in my head, and a dark blue dress that is the right length of classy, yet I already see two areas taunting me—the slit on her skirt and the dip of her cleavage in the front.

Madison's mouth curves into a smirk because she knows she has me. Her ammunition and her mission tonight are to fucking make me contemplate begging.

But that I will not do.

And when she opens her mouth, I'm reminded why this woman provokes me as much as she thrills me.

"Evening, Knox. Ready to work on this collaboration?"

She tilts her head to the side as she waits for me to take in the view of her standing before me.

Helen claps her hands together in pure joy. "You two seem like the perfect pair for all of this. Doesn't she look lovely too?"

Swallowing, I don't take my eyes off Madison. "She looks... like someone who doesn't listen when they're told they don't need to put in much effort."

Helen looks at me in question. "I guess... that's a compliment? Okay, I'll go check on the balloons."

Madison and I don't break our gaze as we are left alone.

"Okay there? Or am I strangling you in your imagination?" Madison greets me.

If only that were true, then maybe my dick would not be struggling to stay down.

"It's going to be a long night, isn't it?" My jaw flexes side to side.

She laughs under her breath. "Excruciatingly long." And it sounds like a promise.

9

MADISON

Staring at a glass of water in front of me, I feel somewhat lost. I don't know where to look because he is everywhere. For the last hour, I've stayed out of Knox's way as he schmoozes my colleagues over wine and cheese. He looks good in dark jeans and a black button-down; it brings out the glint in his sapphire eyes. I'm sure he knows that; every collision of our glances feels like he calculated the effect it would have on me.

His brothers also seem to be influencing people. There is no one here who isn't lapping up their discussion of grapes, pumpkins, or trees. Laughs break out at every joke they spin and every female in the room looks on in a trance.

Ellie is sitting next to me at one of the tables with a mix of teachers. She nudges me. "You okay there? You seem kind of in a daze."

I blink several times, and my attention moves to her. "Totally fine."

"You've barely eaten, I'm not even sure you heard Principal Beal's welcome-back speech, and you insisted on coming alone which means you don't have a designated driver, so you're not drinking. Plus, those glares you and he are throwing at one another are kind of noticeable."

My cheeks tighten from her observation. "Í'm just not feeling this whole evening."

She leans in to speak low as she holds her glass of red in hand. "Our recall of events from last year's prom not doing it for you?"

My lips twist at her reminder. I vaguely recall a story about a cow at prom due to a senior prank, and the star quarterback getting caught with the mayor's daughter.

"Sounded eventful."

"Anyway, we have a solid four months before the seniors get unruly. Right now, they are too scared shitless that they won't get into their college choice."

Blowing out a breath, I couldn't agree more. "Tell me about it. I have a few students retaking the SATs and I'm positive they haven't slept well for weeks."

"Homecoming is late this year, but it will be a relief for them all," Ellie assures me.

Helen arrives at our table and towers over us with a bright smile. "Madison, just wanted to check if you brought the candles for Mr. Laurence? It's his birthday tomorrow, so we were going to sing Happy Birthday." Oh crap, I had no clue it was the science teacher's birthday.

"Candles?"

"Yes, dear, you got the memo? You are helping arrange this evening, after all." Her smile doesn't fade yet her chide is deep in the undertone.

"Am I?" I say to myself, and I'm not sure if she hears me.

She waves a hand at me. "I'm sure Knox can help you. Oh, Knox!" she calls out in an overly chirpy tone that makes me nearly cringe because it may kill my eardrums.

We both look to Knox, standing across the room, who glances up from talking to the music department that are sitting together. When he realizes that he has been summoned, he says something to that table and comes our way, and his smug face is clear.

"Yes, ladies?" he greets us when he arrives to my table.

"Apparently we need candles, birthday candles," I explain with a heavy sigh.

Grayson must have overheard and pipes in to our circle. "I think we have some, I'll go—"

Knox quickly shuts him off by placing his hand against his brother's shoulder. "No worries, I've got this. Plus, I think Ms. Roads, my buddy on this shindig, can help me find them." His attention lands on me, and I can see he is trying to suppress a satisfied grin.

I don't need to divert my gaze to see Grayson look at his brother with an uh-oh-she's-in-trouble look. Or that Ellie on my side is trying to hide her smile by drinking from her glass of wine.

Helen touches Knox's arm. "That's a wonderful idea. While you look for those, do you think you can also bring back some more of those little cracker things? Those are delicious." She squinches her nose and looks like a chipmunk having a field day as her shoulders slant up toward her ears.

Swallowing, I back my chair out in one go and stand. "Let's get this misery over with," I mutter to myself, but I know Knox hears.

Helen walks away, and Grayson gently shakes his head at his brother with a faint smile playing on his lips.

Knox has the audacity to place his hand on the small of my back and instantly something stills inside of me because I think that pumping muscle in my chest needs to adjust.

"Accommodating, as always" he sarcastically tells me as he guides me out of the room until we reach the country-style kitchen that has a few people cooking and placing things in the large fridge, which is fantastic, as it means we are not alone. "This way," he ushers me through the room, and my idea of safe company is now fading away.

"Where are we going?"

He answers by grabbing my wrist and yanking me in through a door and down a few steps into a dimly lit cellar.

Oh. Great.

"Really? Your kidnap plan won't exactly work with the abundance of people here," I say as I jerk my arm away from his hold.

His overly confident smile stretches as he steps forward, causing me to step back until my back lands against a shelf. He leans in, with the heat from his fingers close enough to trace along my body, as he reaches for something behind my head then retrieves it.

"You know, I have a theory about you…" He proudly holds up the pack of birthday candles.

My body arches into his direction, and I can't fight that I want to feel him closer to me.

"What's that?" My voice sounds thick, husky, and I don't quite recognize it.

His tongue licks his lips, and it draws my attention to stare at his mouth. "You don't trust yourself around me, Madison."

"I can handle you just fine, Knox." I remain firm in my pretend belief.

The back of his long finger glides along my arm from my wrist and slowly, agonizingly, and purposefully making a trail up my body, causing heat to spread within me.

"You avoid me, you probably aren't drinking tonight

because you don't trust your inhibitions around me, yet you want me to look at you because why else would you wear a dress like this tonight?" He moves closer to me.

I snicker at his thought. "Please, I avoid you because I feel like I'm allergic to you, and this is how I always dress, nothing wrong with a respectable long-sleeved garment. Not my fault if you can't control your hands."

His upper lip hitches up. "Trust me, Maddie. I'm very controlled, otherwise I'm not entirely sure you would still be in a dress right now."

"Wishful thinking."

Knox's other hand lands on my hip and I flinch from the surprise, though I don't shake him off.

"Was your plan to avoid me all night? Or just until you had a reason to remind me that misery loves company?"

"Shouldn't we get back out there? You seemed to have a fan club in the music department," I simply ask but don't break our eyes connecting.

"They love me because I used to play saxophone way back in the day." He shrugs a shoulder with an almost humorous look.

A chortle escapes me. "What now?" Definitely didn't see that one coming.

"Struggling to comprehend what that means about my blowing skills?"

Exactly.

"Wow, riveting discovery, now shall we go?" I throw on a mundane tone.

"You don't listen, do you? We've been assigned several tasks by Helen, and I have no plans to cause her distress by speeding up what we need to do."

A sound escapes from the back of my throat, as his

sentence is ridiculous. "Crackers and candles, not exactly earth-shattering."

"No, it isn't. But I've already saved your ass by telling Helen that you were a charm to work with and helped with everything for tonight."

I scoff at that. "There was nothing for me to do. Bluetop booster-club tradition, remember? Besides, I *am* a delight, so she doesn't need to be convinced. It's not my fault that your demon powers somehow rub off on me when you are around."

"Fuck, do you ever stop? How do you not exasperate yourself from this? Is it because I haunt your dreams? And I mean the dirty ones, because there is no way we would do anything but hard and deep to the point that you scream."

We stand there in a silence that is causing my entire body to feel like it may explode.

"Would it be fast? Because I'm sure that's all you can deliver, right?" I mock him and tilt my head to side.

"You are kind of insufferable."

"Feeling is mutual."

"Downright exhausting."

I gulp. "Great, we have reached a mutually agreeable conclusion to end this dungeon talk—"

"Just shut up, Madison."

He dips his head down in a quick movement to slam his lips onto my own. My half-second objection fades because the overwhelming urge to give in takes over.

I kiss the jerk back.

Crap.

It only causes him to kiss me deeper, and his tongue encourages my own to come out and play. My tongue is a traitor.

My arms too, because they loop around his neck just as

my mouth moves in a new angle to offer more of myself to him.

The sound of something falling is pure background noise as he presses me against the shelf and his arms tighten around my middle, slightly lifting me in the process.

God, he tastes like expensive wine; it's subtle, but I taste a sweetness mixed with trouble. They should make that into a bottle of Olive Owl wine.

And his lips? A gift, because he knows how to firmly make his objective clear, yet the softness of his lips sends tingles down to my toes.

But his intentions? I don't know.

Mumbling into his mouth and reluctantly trying to pull away from the kiss, the explosion in my mind just has words sputter out. "What the hell?"

"Don't make me quiet you again," he warns me as he murmurs into my neck before he drags his lips down to the base of my throat in that oh-so sensitive spot that makes me want more. Lots more.

"This… this…" I can't speak, and he takes advantage of that by capturing my mouth again, and his hand travels to the back of my head to ensure I stay in place for his damaging kiss.

Somewhere in my head I realize that I am making out with the brother of my student in a cellar, with my new colleagues in the other room.

But I bury it and instead my leg lifts slightly to wrap around his thighs, causing my dress to bunch up to my waist.

What the hell? Why am I turning into a feral animal that needs this man, as if Mother Nature decided that Knox Blisswood is the caveman that I should be attracted to.

Hands are roaming and our kisses are hard and hurried. His gruff chin runs along my neck, and the grazing of his teeth against my skin sends me seeing stars as my head falls back to offer him more, which makes him playfully nip at my skin, and I swear he growls.

Something else falls to the ground and I have no idea the game plan in his head but staying here isn't an option.

With bodies pressed, we both glance to our side to see what fell, and it seems to be a bottle of olive oil that is now a puddle on the ground.

The sound of our heavy breathing fills the room. We look at one another with faces inches apart and maybe panic floods my face but Knox is calm as can be.

His thumb comes up to rub my bottom lip, and I know my mouth must be swollen. "I actually find you tolerable when you're quiet."

I can't say anything as my entire body and mind take in what just transpired.

My eyes finally dare to find his, and this man is confidently satisfied.

"This… this… can't happen again." I try to steady my breathing.

"Are you sure? You seemed to be quite agreeable to this method of communication between us."

My hand comes up to cover my mouth, but really, I want to touch where he has just devoured me, and internally I try to calm my pussy that is squeezing for friction because I am incredibly turned on right now.

"You're trouble," I state.

"For what just happened? Nah, that was 100% mutual."

I break away from our bubble where holding one another feels like a good idea. "Let's just forget this, okay?" I straighten my clothes and hair.

"Not. A. Chance."

"Great, so cooperative yet again," I sarcastically say as I give up on this conversation. "Well, I'm going back to civilization and will see you around." I lean down to pick up the box of candles that must have fallen during our tryst, then turn to march up the steps.

"Don't forget that we have Homecoming next week to work on *together*."

I grumble at his sentence. "By then this evening will have been erased from my mind, I'm sure." I continue on my quest to escape the man, knowing very well I'm doomed.

Already thirty seconds after our indiscretion and I know I'm hooked on his taste and the feeling of his body surrounding me.

When I return to the room filled with Bluetop High's teachers letting loose over food and wine, I think I've pepped myself up enough to get through the next hour or so before faking a headache.

Sliding onto the seat that I had vacated earlier, I grab my glass of water and drink it to try and bring clarity to my thoughts.

"Alright?" Ellie asks.

I hum an okay through my gulp of water.

"Um." She leans in and scans the room as if she wants nobody to listen. "What happened to your neck?"

I spit my water back into my glass, set the drink back on the table, and my hand quickly covers my skin. Sure enough, I feel a sensitive spot.

"It's, uh, nothing. Mosquito."

She gives me a knowing smile. "Right, the kind that just strolled into the room looking like a winner who finally got his prize?"

My eyes dart to Knox who combs a hand through his hair as he approaches Grayson who is pouring some wine for someone.

"What are the chances I can swap your duties? I'll supervise your Saturday detention shift and you can do Homecoming with Satan."

Ellie passes me the breadbasket as if carbs could calm me right now. "Not happening."

Fuck, I need to get a grip.

"Fine. And you're right, it's nothing."

Just because something happens once doesn't mean it will happen again.

MADISON

S taring down at the papers that I'm grading from an earlier class, I'm distracted when Lucy arrives in front of my desk.

"I know," she states.

Inside, I freak out, but only for a hot second. As much as her brother's lips landing on mine has been in my head since the other week, I doubt he would have told his sister. Knox has this sort of mystery that comes with him; although a social guy, he equally seems private. I have no clue what is going on his head, as I haven't received a taunting text like I thought he may send.

So yeah, I doubt he would tell his sister, who he clearly cares deeply for, because that would also disrupt Lucy's focus on college applications and school.

Then again, nothing would surprise me when it comes to Knox Blisswood.

"Oh?" I play dumb.

She nods her head. "I know I should be further ahead with my essays. I mean, each college requests a different subject, so I think I should have at least two done by next week."

Leaning back in my chair, I toss my pen onto the desk. I'm relieved that I can divert my thoughts away from Knox Blisswood, but it still concerns me that Lucy may be stressed.

"Lucy, I promise you are way ahead, and it's fine. You know, sometimes what I do is work really hard during a set period of time, get things done, and then I can relax sooner. As much as spacing out your to-do list is an idea, for some people they work better in shorter periods of time. Is that something you want to try?" I suggest.

A gentle smile forms on her face. "Maybe. I mean, October is quite a busy month for Olive Owl, with pumpkin season, and I guess with Homecoming, it would be nice to just breathe and relax a little."

"You've already handed in two. What, you have two more?"

"Yeah."

"It's possible to do that by the weekend. Set a timer and do a few sprints. I sent you the information on the Pomodoro Technique, and I think you already use it? I was going to assign some homework on Thursday due Friday, but I'll change the deadline to Monday for everyone."

Her bright smile eases me, makes me feel important, more prominently shows me that maybe I am good at what I do.

"Thanks."

The bell rings and soon everyone is hurrying out of the room. Teaching the last class of the day is a mixed bag. On one hand, they've already lost their focus at lunchtime, and on the other hand, they're in good spirits because they know they are almost done for the day.

Sighing, I tidy my desk and prolong leaving because I know my days are numbered. This week I come face to face with Knox again.

We haven't had any communication since I excused myself as soon as dessert was served at the staff dinner. Me and my fake ailment needed to get out of Olive Owl, and my avoidance tactic has worked thus far.

Except, in a few days, we will be thrown together for the sake of hot chocolate and football at the Homecoming game.

My thoughts can't wander too far, because Principal Beal is standing in the doorway to my classroom. The woman should be retiring soon, and for the most part she is the right balance of sweet and stern, depending on the situation, which makes me curious what mood she is in today.

"Madison."

"Good afternoon." I slowly stand as I grab my bag and water bottle. "Everything okay?"

"It is. Actually, I spoke with a few parents at drop-off this morning and they are very pleased with your efforts to help their kids." She walks into the room, yet her tone is neutral.

I try to hide my smile that wants to erupt. "Oh? That's great. I'm happy to help."

"Good. And I think you are putting in effort with extracurricular activities too. Everything seems promising, and of course we will review your work throughout the year."

I swallow a few nerves. "Of course."

Principal Beal touches the small rubber duck sitting on my desk that I got for luck once from a friend in college. "A busy week with Homecoming, and I'm sure we will conquer those Baylor Beavers at the game."

"I hear our team is good this year."

"We are. Even though baseball is our true talent, I think the kids have a chance. I was looking at the volunteer schedule for Homecoming weekend and see you have the game."

I feel uneasy now. "Yes, Helen's orders."

"She knows what she's doing, which is maybe why every year when we vote for the new head of boosters, everyone just votes her back in. Or maybe she rigs the vote, bribing the members with pie, who knows?" Beal brings her hands out and shrugs. "You know Bluetop is small, options are sometimes slim, and even if those options seem like great options, it doesn't mean it's wise. For example, let's say we have a family of prized tomatoes and one of those tomatoes may just be the most phenomenal-tasting thing you ever sank your teeth into… Maybe you just shouldn't."

She lost me with options and tomatoes, but then it quickly sinks in that this is her subtle warning.

"Right," I softly answer and swallow some slight fear. "I don't think it's an issue, as I'm not a fan of the exquisite tomato."

Ms. Beal smiles at me. "Okay then. Just thought I would share some advice for my new favorite teacher."

I only give her a wry smile in response.

"Bye, Madison. Keep up the good work."

Don't ask. Do. Not. Ask.

"Principal Beal?" Shit, I can't resist.

"Yes?"

"Could you maybe tell me why you felt the need to share your tomato philosophy with me?"

She now genuinely smiles at me, as she stands in the doorway with her finger tapping the frame.

"I've lived in this town most of my life. I've watched many students grow up to become men and women. As an educator, you will always have your favorites. It's a lie if a teacher says differently. Just so happens one of my favorites is someone who is single and has a very determined look when he walks around town. I realize that... well... he grew up, and you may just be in his path."

She isn't talking fruit anymore.

"Okay," is all I manage to say.

When she walks off, I feel like the earth just opened to swallow me. My own boss, in the span of a second, subtly confirmed that Knox is both one-of-a-kind and also off-limits. For my own sake, I should stay away to avoid getting hurt.

Which is fine, as I don't need the reminder, because Knox is an irritation to my life, nothing more.

———

MAYBE I SHOULD TAKE Principal Beal's reminder more to heart? It's Friday afternoon, and I'm staring as Knox lifts a barrel onto the table near the bleachers of the football field, and I can't tear my eyes away from Knox's taut biceps that are on display with his Bluetop High jersey, and my imagination has those muscles holding his weight up as he moves on top of me.

Exactly the opposite of what I should be thinking.

As I slowly walk toward my nemesis, he straightens the barrel and glances up at me.

My hands find the back of my jeans pockets, and I stop to stand in front of Knox who has a glint in his eye that is downright sexy. He is trying to read me, but I guess I should just continue with the original plan of pretending nothing ever happened.

"Reporting for duty, so I guess I need your tool."

His brows raise from my words, and already I, too, am regretting my sentence choice.

"I mean, I'm supposed to help decorate the booth, right? I will need tools for that." My lips purse out and I do my best to avoid our eyes encountering one another.

"Sure. Anything else you may need?" He struggles not to let his amusement show.

"Nope." I pop the P.

He indicates with a nod to the pile of supplies on the ground, an abundance of tools and decorations. We both walk over and lean down at the same time, causing our arms to gently graze the other and electricity to spark inside of me.

"So nice of you to join me. I did most of the work already, so it'll be great if you can put in some effort now."

I scoff a sound at his attempt to rile me. "Sorry, I was busy educating our future generation, and one of my students needed extra help, as they have trouble reading."

"Oh." Guilt spreads across his face.

My eyes bulge out at him because I feel like I'm in the right in this moment. Then my view trails down and I realize the number on his jersey. "Really? 69?"

He chuckles, and it sounds sinful, right before he reaches across, causing our shoulders to touch, all so he can grab a roll of tape. "Well yeah, if you and I are going to be selling pumpkin cider and hot chocolate for the big game, then I'm going to wear my Bluetop number 69 jersey from when I was on the football team back in the day. It's tradition." A sheepish grin plays on his mouth. "I know, it turned many heads that I got that number."

Blinking my eyes a few times, I continue past all that. "What happened to saxophone playing?"

He focuses on aligning a few nails on the wood. "You *do* listen. I gave up the sax after junior high. And football? Well, all my brothers played sports. In fact, they will be at the game too in their old jerseys. Lucy fucking hates us for sure on game night, but hey, can't win them all."

Knox now looks at me for a second, standing to tape a sign of prices on the wall of the booth.

"You seem to have this all under control," I say as I look around. "Maybe I'll go collect the cash box from the office, and I need to find my Bluetop shirt."

He quickly steps to me and gently grabs my arm. "Not so fast, shortcake." My eyes peer down to his hand on me, as if he feels he has every right to just touch me whenever he pleases. "Grab it."

My mouth gapes open at his boldness, until his eyes narrow in on me and he seems to catch on that my mind is 100% in the gutter. "The streamer, I mean the streamer," he clarifies.

"Naturally." I step back and take hold of one end of the blue-and-white decoration. We both walk to our ends to hang the string on a hook.

"You handle the cash tonight and I pour the drinks?" he asks.

"Maybe I pour the drinks and you handle the cash."

He steps away from our task and rubs a hand on the back of his neck. "Of course you can't agree with anything I say."

"No, I just think I may be better suited for pouring drinks," I justify and fold my arms, as I feel we may be about to have a standoff.

"I own a winery, I think I can do the drinks."

"I was a bartender in college, so I can handle it just fine."

A closed-mouth smirk dances on his lips, which tells me he is pleasantly annoyed with me right now. "Fine. Was bartending before or after you decided to taint the brains of generation Z?"

"Always wanted to be a teacher since I was little. I had a great teacher in high school who made me decide that those were the grades I wanted to teach. Plus, I taught English as a second language one summer in Ecuador," I explain as I pick up the bag of balloons.

"What a coincidence. I also traveled to Ecuador; three weeks of South America and a backpack."

I feel a flutter in my stomach. This man can't be telling me these things. I don't want to know what similarities we may have, its… dangerous.

"And your tattoo? Was that a souvenir?"

He licks his bottom lip, as I can only assume he enjoys that I've looked at his arms. "No, I got it when my dad was sick a few years ago. He was into cards, poker in particular."

I smile softly at him because he holds onto those memories. "So you always have an ace up your sleeve?"

He strides past me to grab the bag of cups. "I guess I do."

"Crazy Eights is as far as I could go with card games. My dad tried to teach me poker, but I wasn't very good," I explain.

"Your folks live in the suburbs?"

My parents are something I don't particularly like to talk about; it's awkward and complicated. However, for some reason unbeknownst to me, the story easily slides off my lips to Knox's waiting ears. "They do, but I don't see them much. We kind of parted ways… or rather, keep to a once-a-year catch-up conversation and that's it."

"Why is that?" He looks at me with intention to understand.

I tuck some loose hair behind my ear. "My little brother came out as gay his sophomore year of college, and my parents, well, struggled. Until they come around, then I don't feel the need to put in the effort with them. It's been two years. Besides, I've always considered myself closer with my aunt and uncle since my parents sent me there every school vacation because they were busy with work."

"That's not cool. I mean your parents, but sounds like you're okay with your brother?"

"Totally. He lives down in Florida with his boyfriend."

He leans against the table to watch me. "Nice. And here you are stuck in small-town Illinois about to sell warm beverages to overzealous parents. Sounds like everything worked out."

I scoff at his thought as I blow up a balloon with one of those handheld air pumps. "Did it? I'm stuck with you for the next few hours," I remind him.

"Yeah." He walks past me, stopping to stand behind me so he can whisper into my ear. "But now we know what to do when you get out of hand and I need to shut you up."

The reminder sends a warm chill down my body. Up until this moment, we haven't mentioned the other week, but I guess I was naïve to think that Knox would purely let it go.

"Forget it, Knox. Everyone has a moment of bad judgment," I nearly hiss.

I can hear a short laugh as he walks away.

Managing to avoid him for the next two hours, we both do the things we need to do. It doesn't take long for parents to start arriving to get the best seats or students to stand outside the field to paint their faces. So begins our busy shift of continuous sales and chit-chat with customers.

I pour the drinks and Knox collects the money. Other than the occasional glance, things are too hectic to even have the chance to annoy one another.

I'm in my zone of filling red cups that it takes a moment to register the giggle of one of the parents, and looking up, my eyes bug out from the sight of Sophie Plums in full-on makeup, and I can't fucking believe it, a cheerleading outfit.

"So funny that I still have this in my closet, but why not, right? I mean, look at you! Must be great to wear the jersey again. Gosh, those were some good times." Sophie twists her dark hair around her fingers. I catch sight of the giant rock from her husband who is who knows how much older than her. She's giving Knox a flirty look, and I think I may vomit in my mouth from the scene.

Knox nervously laughs, I can hear it. "Times they were." I notice he doesn't mention good.

Ha, take that, Sophie.

"Everything okay? What order am I pouring?" I try to move along the line.

"Oh, hi there, Ms. Roads, I didn't see ya there. What fun, you two doing this together. I'm sure Knox showed you all the ropes." Sophie smiles at me then steps closer to the table between us all and leans over. The back of her hand lands on one side of her mouth to motion that Knox shouldn't hear, then she loudly whispers. "Take it from my experience, if he says he needs to show you something under the bleachers, he means—"

"Okay, and that's that. That was one cider, right?" Knox

quickly cuts in and seems not to be enjoying this situation one bit.

"Right," she chirps back.

"You know, Peter and I are having a little get-together at the house tomorrow since Braden is off to a party. You both should come."

Knox's face tightens and his jaw flexes side to side as the sound of the crowd grumbling due to an almost touchdown fills our ears.

I pour Sophie's cup with a little extra force and hand it to her.

"I'm sure Ms. Roads needs to grade papers," he tells Sophie whose sights haven't left me. She shrugs with a look that he seems to understand, and she takes the cup before walking off.

A hurricane is brewing inside of me, a mixture of jealousy, anger, and confusion. I have no idea what just happened, but I didn't like it.

"Papers to grade? Since when do you speak for me?"

He looks to see that the line has tapered off, before his eyes land on me with intensity and something that feels like possession. "Sorry. By all means, why don't you run along after her and let her know that you will be joining them for their idea of a Saturday night, which includes Chardonnay and *swinging*."

My eyes must be popping out and my jaw drops when I realize he isn't joking.

"Yes, Madison, that's what that invite was," he states again.

"As in you, me, her, him, like swap?" I try to process this.

"Exactly."

But then a button is pushed inside of me that just sets me off, and my only answer is to flee.

"I can't even…" I hold a palm up to stop him from interrupting my internal meltdown before I just leave him and walk away, abandoning my duty and quite possibly my sanity.

———

STORMING down the hallway of the school, there are so many things flying through my head that are bothering me right now.

Knox calling my name doesn't deter me from running.

"Madison, can you wait for a sec?" he calls out.

I cave, and I stop and stand there, feeling him walk to me.

"What are you doing here? Who's watching the stall?" I sound deflated, and I'm being ridiculous among many things right now.

"Grayson and Brooke are, I asked them to."

"Great. Now Helen is going to freak out that we both abandoned our duty." I sigh at this turn of events.

His arm circles around my waist and he quickly ushers me out of the hall through a door. It happens so fast that I don't have time to protest. He turns a light on, and I realize that we are backstage of the vacant auditorium.

"Tell me what the hell is your problem. You give me absolute whiplash." He does sound annoyed, or maybe it's the fact that there isn't much distance between us which causes us to sense more of each other. Our breath, our chests heaving, and our eyes unable to look away from the other. Everything is more intense, more inescapable.

"My problem?" My hands go out in frustration. "You

are completely bad news, Knox, being around you is bad news. In the span of days, I've been warned off you because Principal Beal, my boss, seems to think that you and I may have a potential click and heaven help me that I may not be worthy of her beloved student, which is insanity. Then I have your crazy high school ex, who thinks that you and I are together, then invites me to swing with her and her husband. By association, none of this puts me in a good position."

His face looks confused. "Principal Beal warned you off me?" Then his proud smug smirk comes out. "That old devil."

I roll my eyes and shake my head; he doesn't get the point.

"And ignore Sophie. She's always been a little out there, and I have never given her any indication that there is a possibility to have another round on this saddle."

"Ugh. The fact I even heard that sentence reminds me how breathing the same air as you is infuriating." My hands comb through my hair and I grab some to let out some stress.

"You know you really need to take a chill pill. Since day one you have only been judgmental, uptight, and extremely moody around me. And I have no goddamn clue why I find it so fucking attractive too."

"Attractive?" I admit that his declaration causes me to dance somewhere inside.

He tips his chin down as if he suddenly could go shy that he admitted it out loud. "And stubborn."

"Why did you follow me?"

His hands rub the back of his neck. "Figured getting asked to a small-town swinger's party might have knocked you off your axis a little."

"I'm not some prim-and-proper lady, Knox. That isn't what shocked me. I just can't have people assuming I'm together with my student's..." Parent, guardian, brother... their family situation is complicated, and I am sensitive to that.

His hand comes to cup my face, and he draws me closer to him so our bodies are inches apart. "If you are not a well-behaved soul, then what are you?"

My breath grows heavy, and when I close my eyes for a second to collect my bearings and thoughts, I can't escape.

"A stupid one maybe for getting stuck alone with you." I feel something build inside of me that wants to explode.

"Right, because heaven forbid you actually have something nice to say to me. Your Knox-is-the-bad-guy routine is really getting old. Those cement walls you build really are making this so damn uneasy—"

"Shut up," I demand before I crash my lips onto his.

KNOX

Kiss her back.

Don't let her lead. Madison may have started this round but I'm going to show her who is boss. But hot damn, I'm curious what she's like when she's in control.

Both of my hands cradle her face as I decide to devour her mouth.

My curiosity is going to have to wait. I've never been a patient man, and right now I want to kiss her senseless.

She murmurs and it gets lost somewhere in my breath, right before I tilt her head back slightly to angle her for a better position. Those hands of hers, that somehow are clinging to my jersey as if her life depended on it, now slide up around my neck, because it seems she is enjoying this.

All indications are that I should pull her closer, feel her against me, and it causes my dick to feel misery because I can't screw this woman at her place of work.

"Damn it, I do stupid stuff around you," she seems to

scold herself when we capture a breath before she returns her lips to mine.

But I can't let that comment go.

Against her lips, I taunt her with a fact. "This time is all your initiation."

"Shh," she berates me.

I grin against her chin before we meet again for a deep long kiss, with my tongue swiping into her mouth, and she tastes of hot chocolate. So sweet, addictively sweet, and it will linger on my tastebuds for sure.

My hands travel down to her ass, and she yelps a soft surprise when I squeeze her cheeks through the jeans, but it's a pleasant surprise because she only presses her body into mine.

This is torment. What am I supposed to do with her? I can't exactly take her on the floor or against the wall here. And by the time I convince her to go somewhere else, I'm sure her crazy mind will talk her out of it.

All I can do is enjoy this.

Madison quiet.

Because of a kiss.

A kiss she started.

I'm never letting that go.

Her hands roam down, and I am curious what she's up to, but then her hands travel up and under my shirt and I realize she is feeling my abs.

A good choice for exploration but would have preferred if she aimed a little lower.

We kiss, and kiss more. Until our arms and hands return to somewhat respectable positions.

Well, until Madison begins to freak out, which I already saw coming, because really, it's Madison, so nothing will be simple.

She begins to pull away from my lips, but reluctantly. It takes several attempted releases, then repeat kisses, until she finally retreats, and her fingers find her lips to touch to ensure she didn't just dream the best kiss of her life.

"Wh-what just happened?" she whispers in a sort of shock, and her eyes don't blink.

"Our method, I guess."

"I swear to God you possess me when you're around, and I'll start speaking tongues or something soon." Her hand runs along her cheek until her head rests against it.

My jaw ticks from her determination to keep up this charade. "Well… we know what to do so you don't speak."

She points a finger at me. "You!"

"Nope. Nuh-uh." I'm going to stand my ground. "It takes two to tango, lady. I'm not taking the blame for your need to harass me, in the school auditorium no less."

Madison looks around and something sinks in or clicks, because she laughs then looks up at me with a sort of honesty that gives me the feeling that maybe I've finally chipped away part of her wall.

"Mistakes can happen twice. I mean, it's not like this is the third time. Then that would be a development, not a mistake," she rambles some philosophy, but to my ears, it's an invitation for another round.

"Sure. Now, are you okay?" I throw my arm around her shoulders to guide her back out into civilization—*sadly*. "I mean, as much as this has been fun, we should probably head back out."

She allows me to tow her along, as she seems slightly in a daze, which isn't the first time that I've had that effect on someone.

"Now you want to be responsible? You just happened to know where to hide us for the last ten minutes?" She doubts me, and it's fair, I may have known we would undoubtedly have some privacy backstage.

As much as it's fun to pull out the tricks from my teenage years, that isn't who I am now. I'm a grown man. One who, looking at Madison, I can't seem to run away from. I'm the man who is too intrigued by the woman who throws me snarled looks and kisses me like it means something.

I wonder if she will go home tonight and congratulate herself for making an adult man feel like a puppy who is waiting for a treat.

"Knox." The way she says my name sounds promising, or rather it's not laced with disdain for once.

"Yes, shortcake?" I continue to look forward as we approach the parking lot, and I let my arm drop from around her as we walk.

"Please don't breathe a word of this again tonight," she requests.

Smirking, I promise. "Sure… but you only said tonight. Next week I may have to remind you that your hands were all too eager."

"Well… if I was going to make the mistake then I might as well enjoy it. So what if my hands decided to feel up your rock-hard abs, which I need to ask, what the hell do you do to make that happen? Like, really?"

"Maddie, you just used enjoy and me in the same sentence. That's what I call progress."

I turn to look at her and the most beautiful of gentlest smiles dances on her lips before she traps her bottom lip between her teeth.

It seems she knows that I'm not wrong.

And more surprisingly, she doesn't seem concerned by that.

———

AFTER WE RETURNED to our duty at the stall, the night went quickly, and soon we went our separate ways. I had some old buddies in town that I wanted to see, so my weekend was busy. Over the next week, I had to go to Chicago for a delivery, and pumpkin season meant all hands on deck at Olive Owl.

By the end of the week, I couldn't resist and had to deliver on my promise. I sent Madison a text.

Me: Remember the time you said second time is still a mistake? Happy one week yeah-you-totally-kissed-me anniversary.

It doesn't take long for her to respond either.

Madison: Who is this? I vaguely recognize the number as this guy who is a total douche and checks out women's asses in the chip aisle, but I'm not sure.

Me: Really? Circling us back to that?

She sends back a smiley face with sunglasses.

Me: Hope they're out of chocolate pretzels next time you're there.

Madison: See? I knew you were the devil.

Me: Any plans this weekend other than your hand and your book?

Madison: Cute. And no plans as I have to monitor the SATS this weekend. Poor kids.

Me: Yikes. Have fun, and if you need someone to save you, well, you know... you've felt my muscles.

She sends back a middle finger, but I like her a little crass.

———

THE FEW WEEKS after that are again busy days, and I'm relieved when I make it to Rooster Sin for Friday-night live music. Drew is playing an acoustic set, so it's a perfect excuse to have a night off.

Drinking from my bottle of beer, I sit at the bar and look around at the ambience of the hole-in-the-wall institution of Bluetop. Tonight there are remnants of popcorn on the ground, with probably a weeks' worth of spilled beer, but everyone is having a good time in the low-lit place with a jukebox in one corner and green lighting for the little podium.

Bennett looks at me as he throws a piece of popcorn into his mouth. "He's really getting good. Did he write these songs himself?" Bennett asks and indicates to Drew who is retuning his guitar between sets.

"Yeah. Guitar, boxing, and construction, that's Drew. Good for him for performing in public," I comment and scan the busy room, maybe because I wonder if tonight is another chance encounter with the woman of my contempt.

"Maybe I should ask him to play at the holiday party this year at Olive Owl. Or ask if he wants to do a few wedding receptions."

I laugh at his suggestion. "That guy there has talent. I'm not sure wedding receptions are his calling."

"Okay, and? That one wedding back in June flew in some country star. Olive Owl isn't just a wedding reception destination, it's the place to be," he proudly reminds me.

I slap a hand on his back as I smile, since I couldn't agree more.

The door opens and my head perks up to see a woman in her forties enter Rooster Sin.

"Hoping to become teacher's pet tonight?" Bennett side-eyes me.

"Why would you think that?"

"Well, considering Grayson and I figured out what you got up to at the Homecoming game, then I'm kind of surprised that there haven't been any developments," he explains. The moment Madison left that night, Grayson and Bennett were on me because apparently I had *that* look. And I have no reason to lie to them.

I play with the paper label of the beer bottle as I admit, "We've both been kind of busy, and I'm not sure she has thawed enough of the iciness yet when it comes to me or the fact she is Lucy's teacher."

Bennett scratches the stubble on his cheek. "Ah, right, that. A bit murky, but I guess who the fuck cares. What Lucy doesn't know won't kill her."

My eyes widen at his casual response to it.

He shrugs at my reaction. "Knox, you actually seem, I don't know, in a lighter mood lately. Hell, did you actually whistle the other day on the farm? You're losing your grumpy touch. I think that's worth exploration because I think it has to do with a certain woman. Grayson would say the same thing."

"Because you both ended up with who you were meant to be with, and you're now tied down for life with kids, and I'm waiting on word that you got a puppy or something too," I joke, but underneath it lies truth. Maybe even a ping of jealousy too—they're not alone.

The crowd begins to clap as Drew sits down again on the stool behind a mic.

I clap my hands together in support, and he begins to strum the strings of his instrument. In the corner of my eye, I see movement, and my head shoots to the door that opens.

To Madison.

Who looks… like a beautiful wreck.

She walks straight to the bar and lands next to Bennett and me, but she is oblivious as she requests a 0% beer. Despite her dress that she must have worn to school. It's too pretty for a place like this, yet casual enough, though it doesn't distract me from the fact that she has a square bandage on her forehead.

"Fuck, what happened?" I can't hide my concern.

Madison looks up at both of us. "Oh... hey."

"You okay?" Bennett asks her, then looks at me to double-check that I'm witnessing the fact that Madison is missing her usual voltage of feistiness around me.

"Oh, you mean this?" She points to her head. "I guess Lucy didn't mention it. Hazards of the job, I guess." Madison shrugs and gives a polite nod to the bartender who places a beer in front of her.

Bennett touches my arm and lets me know that he's going to head somewhere else in the bar, giving me the opportunity to slide closer to Madison.

"What the hell happened?"

"Two juniors got in a fight in the hallway yesterday, and I tried to split them up. Unfortunately, a sixteen-year-old wrestler is a lot stronger than you may think, and he accidently shoved me into the trophy cabinet. I mean, they say it isn't a concussion, so it should be fine. The other boy looked a hell of a lot worse." She brushes it all off like it's a normal day at the office.

"Uhm, I'm positive that's not what you signed up for when you became a teacher. What in the world were they fighting about?"

She gives me a do-you-even-need-to-ask look. "A girl, of course. What else would make their testosterone skyrocket?" She drinks from the bottle and looks back at the podium to Drew playing.

"And you came here to unwind?" I pry for details.

She glances at me and smirks. "I mean, I wasn't planning on you being here, as that kind of defeats my relax and destress scenario that I had going."

"Sorry to disappoint."

"It's okay. I kind of legit lost my energy to quarrel with you today. So that option is at a level zero."

"Lucky me."

Our eyes lock as small grins form on both of our faces before we focus on the music.

Drinking my beer, I hear the song, but all my awareness is on the fact that Madison is sitting next to me and our arms graze as we both lean against the bar.

"How did you come here?" I ask.

"Ellie dropped me off on her way home, and I'll figure out a way back to my place. I just needed an hour of something different than my couch."

"Good. I'll take you. I mean home," I confidently tell her.

She swallows a giant sip of beer and takes a moment to consider. "Oh... I'm sure someone else can do it."

"It's fine. I have to be up at 6am, so don't you worry, the big bad wolf won't sleep over."

Madison sputters out her beer then drags the back of her hand across her mouth. "You wouldn't get an invitation, so you're fine."

"Settled then."

"Sure," she echoes back.

———

AFTER ONE MORE SONG FROM Drew, Madison and I both easily agreed to go. Almost eagerly, as if we both wanted to get out of there to chase our curiosity.

The car ride back is quiet and maybe she's nervous, which would make sense, as I'm clueless how to proceed with the night because there has been a shift between us since we last saw one another.

When we reach her apartment complex, I turn the engine off. She slowly unbuckles her seatbelt but doesn't bounce out of her seat to bid me adieu, which only causes me to turn to her in my seat to focus on her, because I feel like she wants this moment to linger.

"You okay?" I ask, and I mean it genuinely.

She pinches the bridge of her nose. "I guess that hit-in-the-head headache is coming on. I think I have an Advil somewhere or something."

"Something?" The light from the parking lot and dashboard allows me to see her blush, and now I'm intrigued. "What is the other option?"

Her mouth opens and she debates speaking as she leans back in her seat. "I just meant there are ways to relieve a headache."

I slide closer to the middle console. "Ways? Such as?" It trails off my tongue.

She tightly smiles at me as I move slowly closer, and she swallows as her eyes dart down to the proud erection happening in my pants. "It's a proven fact that certain... *acts* relieve headaches... I don't need your help for that."

My fingers trace the shape of her knee before gliding up her thin layer of tights and land on her thigh as if she is already mine to touch. "I wasn't offering, shortcake, but do explain further."

"Knox, I feel like a ton of bricks hit me. So be it if I

decide to give myself an orgasm to try and relieve my head, and yes, I did just say that, because despite what you thought that one night, I'm not afraid to talk about sex." She glances down at my hand touching her.

No, you're a confident vixen sent to this earth to bring me to my knees.

"Let me help you get rid of that headache," I state as I tip my head in the direction of my hand moving up and agonizing us both. I know that my eyes are hazed with adamancy.

A sultry look spreads across her face. "What are you doing?" She's coy and amused.

My fingers reach destination waistband of her tights under her skirt that is now bunched at her waist. I then pause. "I already feel that you're intrigued." She's warm.

I wait for her to object, but she doesn't. Instead, I venture inside of her tights and her breath hitches. Her face freezes with a curious look as I slide a finger through her folds and her mouth parts open.

"This is a horrible idea." She smiles with an audible breath. "But if you feel you have a point to prove, then who am I to stop your efforts." She playfully speaks in a sexy tone as I popcorn kisses along her neck, and I deliberately slowly stroke her.

"Shh, we like you quiet, remember?" Another kiss against her silky skin that smells of watermelon.

"I don't listen, *remember*?" Her breath grows heavy as my mouth inches closer to her own.

She is entirely bare down there, and her juices coat my finger that I drag up to circle her clit, causing her to gasp. It ignites a need inside of me to kiss her mouth.

Madison's hips buck up to use my hand as friction as she offers me her tongue in my mouth, along with a moan.

Dipping another finger inside of her, I feel how incredibly tight she is, and a moan escapes her as our eyes meet and foreheads touch.

"Shh," I tease her before I pick up my rhythm.

She rides my fingers as she grips my wrist that is resting against her pelvis, I see that she is watching my every move.

Between my fingers and another kiss, I'll make her see stars.

"Knox," she cries out my name as her head falls onto my shoulder and her hair smells of cotton candy, fantastic.

Her thighs spread farther open as she arches up against me, which in turn makes me go relentless to relieve her.

A few circles more on her little bud and I feel her trembling under me, but I can't stop. I want to feel every second of what I have accomplished, and my fingers stay on her until she calms and breathes out a long *whoa*.

Pulling my hand out from under her waistband, I watch her sit there, flushed and in a state of pleasure.

"Headache gone?" I ask with a cheeky look. My fingers come to my mouth, but she quickly captures my wrist, and with her eyes in a fixed stare with my own, she offers me my own fingers soaked in her arousal and brings it to my mouth to watch me suck my fingers for a taste. Sweet and addictive, my senses may have discovered a new tastebud.

And fucking hell, she is hot right now.

Then to knock me off balance, she leans in, desperate for my kiss, and tries to take all she can get.

She pulls back, with her thumb rubbing a circle against my cheek. "I feel far better."

Her other hand gropes the situation happening under my zipper, but this isn't tit for tat, so I grab her forearm and pull her away. "Next time, Maddie. You need to rest, and I should get home."

She gives me a mischievous grin. "You're confident that there will be a next time."

I kiss her forehead before leaning over to pull on the latch of the car door. "We just fooled around in the front seat of my car—"

"How ridiculous of us," she nonchalantly replies, and I hear the humor, because so far, we have found ourselves in settings fit for horny teenagers.

"I believe a wise person once said twice is a mistake, but a third time is a development. I'm sure you can count." I wink at her.

She blushes and bites her inner cheek to control her smile. "I'm too under the influence of orgasm endorphins to argue with you right now."

"Well, when you're out of your spell, then the ball is in your court, Madison." I get the door open.

And that's where we leave things.

12

MADISON

itting at Bear Brew, the coffee spot that is my little sanctuary at 4pm on a Tuesday while I plan my classes for the upcoming weeks, I type away on my laptop and drink tea in between pauses.

It's not busy, so it is very easy to spot when someone comes through the door. What I'm not anticipating is Knox to arrive with a baby in his arms.

Not only have I avoided him for the last week since he made me come in his car, but I've been in a constant debate with myself about whether I should text him or not. I'm equal parts annoyed that I keep having indiscretions with him, but damn it, a smile tugs on my mouth at the thought of him.

And here he is.

With a baby.

In one of those carrier things strapped to his body, and he's cooing with the child. My legs cross and tighten under the table, as this is an unexpected view that isn't half bad.

His eyes land on me and he seems surprised to see me,

but he isn't going to avoid me, so he walks over. "Well, isn't this going to be fun."

"Hello to you too. Who's your friend?" I indicate with my head to the baby with chubby cheeks, and I smile because I can't suppress that I'm pleasantly okay with this unforeseen meet-up.

Knox sits on the chair at the other side of the table and unclicks the carrier to circle the baby around to sitting on his lap. "This is my nephew, J.J. Bennett needed to run an errand and Kelsey still has another appointment at her salon, so Uncle Knox was roped into babysitting."

The baby squeals and it's freaking adorable. "I see. I didn't take you for the babysitting type."

"I'm only allowed up to half-hour increments, otherwise it turns into a disaster since I'm not made for babysitting," he admits, and it's both honest and funny. Knox motions to the person behind the counter for a coffee, and I can only assume they know his order by heart. "Throw in a piece of fruit or cookie or something for the kid," he also requests.

His attention turns to me, and I bring my mug of tea to my lips, unsure of what to say. "So... my head is better."

"I can see the bandage is gone. Lucy mentioned the boys were suspended for a few days."

"Yeah, for fighting. I wasn't going to make a deal out of my head. Besides, I think the battle scar gave me a good street rep with my students."

He grins at me. "Does it mean your memory is fine?"

"Very." I set my mug down on the table. "Crystal clear, actually."

"Oh?" His brows knit together, and before we can continue, his order is brought to the table, and he thanks the barista. "You just choose to forget it," he states casually as he shakes a packet of sugar and pours it into his cup.

"No. I just… need to figure out my strategy for dealing with you."

"I have a few recommendations."

"I'm sure you do," I say and help him break the granola bar into pieces for his nephew.

He places his hands over his nephew's ears. "Look, I'm not that irresponsible. It probably isn't the right time for a discussion of how your sexual frustration makes you a tough cookie to deal with. I mean, we have young ears at the table." Knox releases his hands from the baby's head. "So let's have a normal civil conversation, Madison. Let's see how you respond to that, or is it you only get excited when you picture devil horns coming from my head?"

"We can try. I mean, I haven't exactly packed up and left yet, have I?"

He bounces J.J. on his lap. "Good. Tell me, what are you working on?"

"I'm making course plans for the coming weeks. I'm actually teaching English as a second language at night, I do that once a week. It's volunteer, but it's important, as some of my students are trying to find better jobs."

"A good Samaritan. You do that in Bluetop?"

"Yeah, at the high school. See, I am busy, that isn't a lie."

He glances away then returns his gaze to me and scratches the thin layer of scruff on his chin, which draws my thoughts to a time when his hand was worshipping my pussy as if he was possessed by me.

"That's why you haven't yet invited me over for a homecooked meal with a side of attitude?"

My lips purse out, as I know I'm supposed to take the lead. "Right, ball in my court."

He sips his coffee as he stares at me. "Exactly. I don't chase, Maddie, I have no reason to."

I huff at his arrogance. "Sure, because every female just comes running to you."

"No. It's because I think you should find your way on your own terms. I'm not going to –"

"Knox, there you are!"

Both of our heads whip to the direction of the door and we see Lucy walking in.

"I've been sent to relieve you from babysitting duty, since, well… we don't trust you, not since you thought it would be funny to dress him up as a pirate and drew a mustache on him."

"Hey, it was a cute photo, and I didn't know it was permanent marker. Plus, it came off… eventually."

Lucy rolls her eyes, then looks to me, and then between Knox and me. "Oh, hi, Ms. Roads, I didn't know you would be here. What are you two talking about?" she asks innocently as she grabs her nephew.

"We are… discussing…" My brain freezes.

"Oh, is this you two discussing my chances of getting accepted to my top picks?"

"Lucy, you need to chill. Not everything is about college," Knox reminds her, and it isn't to divert the topic, but more from a place of concern.

"I'm sure Lucy is just excited for the weeks ahead." I send a warning glare to Knox to ease up, then I turn my focus to Lucy. "Maybe your brother has a point. You handed in all your applications last week. There is nothing you can do while you wait except relax and enjoy life," I suggest as I pack up my notebook and laptop.

Lucy looks between us. "I guess. Knox wasn't bothering you, was he? Please know that I am in no way a reflection of his lack of positive qualities, but surprisingly, he has a few okay-ish attributes."

I laugh at her sentence that only a sister would say, as teasing your brother is a natural instinct.

"Thanks, Lucy. You really make me feel great," he sarcastically replies. "I've been perfectly *giving* to your favorite teacher."

I shoot him an unimpressed look. "Trust me, everything is fine."

"Oh good. So, what were you two talking about?" she inquires again.

"Waiting. I explained to Ms. Roads about Olive Owl wine and how certain grapes don't do well with the waiting process and just don't do well all packaged up."

Lucy looks between us, skeptical, but seems to roll with it.

I swallow as I stand to pack up my bag. "Funny. I thought the longer the wait the better they taste?" The tick of his jaw tells me he is satisfied with my remark. "Anyway, I should go. It was good running into you all, including the little munchkin." My nose tips in the direction of their nephew. "See you tomorrow in class, Lucy."

"Sure," she answers.

My eyes dart to Knox who looks at me with intent, and I wish we were both mind-readers.

But alas, we are not.

———

I'M off to see my aunt and uncle for the weekend for Thanksgiving, which will be a good escape. It will be my first time away from Bluetop since I moved, and a change of scenery may help clear my senses.

I sigh as I drive along the road on this gray late afternoon, very well aware that I'll need to drive past Olive Owl and that I still haven't made any steps that would put me in Knox's good books.

I've actually avoided him.

He may think it's because I'm not interested, but I call it protection against an unknown.

There is a way about him that has me uneasy. He's exhilarating and frustrating, but most of all, I'm not sure it's possible to kiss him again and not want more. And I don't mean get naked and have a long night kind of more, because that alone is enticing. But no, there is some inclination inside of me that he may hook me into something that I haven't experienced before.

And Knox Blisswood doesn't chase.

He certainly kept his word on that too, as it's been radio silence from him. Granted, I haven't texted since the other week after our run-in.

Looking ahead on the road, my journey out of town doesn't last long. My eyes spot movement on the edge of the road and instinct has me move my wheel to swerve and slam on the brakes.

My car comes to a screeching halt, avoiding an accident, and when the shock wears off, I scan my body to realize nothing has happened. Quickly unbuckling my seatbelt, I get out of my car to check what the hell just happened.

I blink my eyes a few times to see what I missed hitting with my car, and it doesn't take long to see what caught my eye, and I know that I will need help.

Blowing out a breath, I realize that I have no choice but

to see the man I was escaping.

13

KNOX

The sound of a knock on the door confuses me. My brothers are out completing errands that their wives sent them on to prepare for Thanksgiving tomorrow, and Drew just left for the day. We're not expecting any guests either, which is why the front door was locked.

When I open the door, I'm surprised to find Madison standing there. As much as I wonder if this is her finally making her move in our game of chess, her look has me feeling that I may not like this conversation.

"Hi," she greets me, and it feels kind of awkward.

"Hi." I wait for her to continue because I'm not going to lead this conversation.

"I need your help," she states, and her face looks uneasy.

I lean against the inner pane of the front door. I'm not going to drop to my knees and be her hero right now. "Wow, ballsy. You have ghosted me for a few weeks and the first thing you do is ask for my help."

Her face drops and guilt washes over her. "I know.

You're right, I should have reached out. I've been busy and…"

"Message clear." I cross my arms over my chest, and truthfully, I think I may be scared that for once I'm on the receiving end of the "it's not you, it's me" conversation.

Her hand comes out to touch my arm. "No! I mean, well, I don't know what I mean. I just need your help."

My eyes study her for a second and I can see she is conflicted, which causes me to internally weaken.

"I was driving on my way out of town, and I swerved my car to avoid hitting a dog—"

"Shit." My arms flop to my sides and I straighten my posture as I now look all over her body intently, but her winter coat doesn't help me assess if she has been hurt.

"I'm fine. Car is fine. But the dog—"

My voice fills with dread. "Oh no. Tell me there isn't roadkill."

"No, there isn't. But the thing is, I couldn't just leave him there on the side of the road, the stray dog I mean." She attempts an awkward smile, and I now wonder what she is asking of me.

"Okay, and?"

"It's the night before Thanksgiving, so the shelter is closed, but I wouldn't want him to go there anyway if they don't have space, then who knows what would happen to him, plus maybe he has a home or maybe he ends up in a cage at the shelter and, you know, all those families go away during the holidays, only not really thinking about the responsibilities. I would love to take him with me, but I need to drive down to my aunt and uncle's place, plus my apartment doesn't allow dogs. But it's supposed to get cold, so he needs a place to stay—"

I smile tightly as her adorable-as-fuck rambling is

enough information for me to realize what she's asking. "Let me guess, you thought he could stay here?"

"At least until I manage to start looking for his owners." Her eyes are pleading.

I bitterly laugh at this unexpected day. "Madison, you avoid me, only to come to me to help you out of your predicament. You have some nerve."

"What?" She seems flabbergasted by my prodding jab. "Can we not go into the whole story of you looking at my ass, kissing me in a cellar, then behind the stage, oh and making me lose my damn mind in the front of your car?"

I step to her now, ready to challenge her. "Excuse me, but this is not all on me. *You* kissed me that one time, and *you* were more than willing to come on my hand. Besides, we are at the development stage now, *you* just choose to do nothing."

Her hands comb through her hair and she bites her lip. She is clearly swallowing her desire to debate me some more.

"Knox, you're right. Okay? There, I said it. You're right. But in this moment, can we just focus on the dog?" she begs as our eyes meet.

"Right, because you need me to be the hero. Where is this dog?" I ask her and rub my forehead from this situation.

Right on cue, the sound of a dog yawning draws our attention to the left.

How the hell did I miss this?

"Are you joking?" I ask Madison.

She shrugs. "He's beautiful and seems really sweet."

I point to the giant dog with brown, white, and black fur. His paws would easily fill the palm of my hand. "This isn't a dog. This is half a Cosmo, the horse."

The dog sits obediently, panting breath, and he has drool falling from one side of his mouth.

"I mean, he *is* a larger dog. A Bernese Mountain dog, actually. They love winter and are working dogs. I'm sure he will fit right in here at Olive Owl," she attempts to convince me of the fact she has delivered a canine that may weigh as much as Madison herself to my doorstep.

Leaning down, I can't help it but pet the beast, who whimpers a sound of approval that I'm giving him attention.

"I'll be back by the end of the weekend and will come up with a plan. Maybe I can phone a rescue group or something. Just please, he was on the side of the road."

"He could have rabies or kill me during my sleep for all we know."

Madison leans down and begins to rub the dog's face. "You wouldn't dare. You're a good boy, aren't you?" she coos to the animal.

Standing back up, I sigh. He gives her his paw as if he knows showing off his skills would sway my decision.

"Fine. But you better come back by the end of the weekend with a plan, and if I find a solution for the creature before then, I will send him off." Truthfully, I'm not going to put in any effort to find him a home, but I need to show them both who is in charge, because right now I feel like they both can walk over me with cuteness and tricks.

Madison jumps up and her worries disappear, along with her invisible wall she had up between us, as she throws her arms around my neck, and my own arms wrap around her middle like they've landed home. She feels too damn good in my hold, a fit like no other.

"Thank you, Knox."

"He can stay in the barn with Cosmo." I try to keep up my disdain for this situation, but I already know he is getting an invite to the house since he does look like a kickass dog.

Her arms fall to her sides, and she steps back to study my face. "Okay, and I mean, just make sure he gets water and food."

"I literally run a winery; I think I know what it entails to keep a living organism alive."

The corners of her mouth lift from my attitude. "Again, thank you."

"You won't be thanking me when I come to collect my reward." It comes out of my mouth, when in reality a dirty thought flashes through my head of what I should make her do to show her gratitude.

She licks her lips and tucks a few loose strands of hair behind her ear. "I think I can handle it."

We look at one another as a thick moment of silence hits us. We both must feel this magnetic connection that we can't deny, which only in turn makes me furious that she hasn't made a move in the last few weeks.

"I should go," she softly mentions.

"Sure. We're used to this by now, right? I mean, we only see each other by accident and not by plan."

She gulps and must feel the heat of my gaze then shakes her head. "Bye, Knox. I'll be back after the weekend... that *is* by plan." She raises a brow at me to show she has a point to prove, before she pivots with a bit of snark, which is just the way I like her.

"You're welcome, by the way!" I call out to her as she heads off to her car.

Looking down at the dog, his eyes are like two daggers to the soul. He seems as though he knows that he is being used as an emotional pawn in my romantic life and is happy to be along for the ride.

I groan out my exhaustion of how that woman has me by the balls, and truthfully, I'm waiting for her. I am secretly begging for her to come around. Everything that I swore I would never do, I want to try with someone.

Every time Madison and I cross paths, she brings a bag of mixed signals. Maybe I should cut the rope that she has no clue I'm holding onto, or maybe I should just wait a little longer.

Because for the first time in my life, I hope for something good with someone. And that someone is the woman who just showed up on my step with a dog that I am now responsible for, and a promise that she will return.

Is it crazy that it feels like she may just come back for me?

14

MADISON

I flop my overfilled turkey sandwich onto the plate. Leftovers from Thanksgiving are normally my favorite—you can't really go wrong with a turkey sandwich filled with cranberry sauce, and a slice of pumpkin pie for dessert. It just seems to age better by the day.

"Honey, you've been very distracted since you arrived Wednesday night. Is it the dog?" Aunt Carol asks me as she redistributes stuffing into new plastic containers.

I think about what she asked, scratching the back of my head. It's so many things. "I'm sure Knox is taking care of him." Because I know underneath his steely exterior that he cares for actual living things.

Yesterday, I had Thanksgiving dinner with my aunt and uncle. They invited a few neighbors over, and it was the usual meal that we have every year, my aunt's pecan clusters included.

My aunt smiles at me, and I notice her eyes indicate that she has something to share. "Tell me more about Knox."

Oh, it's the interrogation round.

"He is a bit of a nuisance, not exactly easy to deal with, and I can't really escape him. His sister is my student. Their parents passed, so she lives with their oldest brother, but they all kind of team up to watch out for her. Kind of sweet, really."

"A nuisance can be good. Keeps you on your toes," she mentions as she continues her quest to reorganize the kitchen counter.

I nibble on a piece of turkey. "That he does," I mumble then look at my phone for any news from Mr. Trouble himself—nothing. The only thing I see is a notification on the weather.

"Sweety, you've been daydreaming since you got here. I doubt it's the dog, so tell me what is really bothering you."

I never could hide my true feelings from my aunt. She was there when I got my first period and my mom was too busy with a work function. My aunt was also there when I went off to college.

"We keep circling each other," I begin to assess my situation. "Didn't start off on the right foot, in fact the wrong foot from moment one. But… I'm not sure it was that wrong after all. There's a spark, maybe. I just don't know how to handle it. Besides, it's complicated since his sister is my student, and I'm not sure if Knox and I are anything but a flirtation."

My aunt closes the fridge and leans over the counter. "But the heart wants what it wants, and how do you know if you don't explore further?"

"It's risky," I lament.

"For your work or for your heart? Because the Madison I know wouldn't let obstacles get in her way."

I look at her, and debate with myself if I can finally admit the truth. "You're right. I guess I'm scared. What happens if we... discover more about one another?"

"What's the worst that can happen? You realize that you have nothing in common, *or...* he could be everything you've always wanted."

I blow out a breath. I hate how people are wiser when they're older. "It could be just attraction. Opposites attract, right?"

She laughs at me as she traps my hand between her own. "Sounds like you two aren't opposites at all, otherwise why would you keep circling one another?"

"He said it's my turn to make a move, that he doesn't chase or beg for anyone. After all, Knox Blisswood has a whole list of women ready at his beck and call." It annoys me, that philosophy.

"Jealous? Anyway, you will see him soon and probably owe him more conversation than just thanks for saving the dog. Does he know it's your dream dog?"

I laugh at the suggestion. "What was I going to say? 'Hey, Knox, I know we annoy one another, and you are probably ready to cut me off, but please, please watch this dog, which by the way is my favorite breed and I've dreamed about having this very type of dog, along with a house with land to farm on.'" I press my hands together and pretend to beg.

"It's a sign from above."

Standing up, I walk to the kitchen window to look outside. A snowstorm is on the way, according to reports.

"Anyway, I have a few more days to figure it out."

"Go now."

I turn around to look at my aunt, and I'm puzzled, as I said I would stay until Sunday.

"We love having you here, but you've been staring at your phone every five minutes. Plus, with the snow expected, then it is probably better to head out before the roads get messy," Aunt Carol explains, and what she says does make sense.

"The roads, right."

"That's one thing, but I think there is a young man who is probably fighting his internal thoughts too."

I smile to myself. "Ah, is this a push?"

"Nah, honey, you already know what you want, you're just overthinking it. But maybe sometimes you shouldn't think at all."

Walking to her, I hug her, because she's right. I just need to take a step… or a giant leap.

———

Two hours later, I reach Olive Owl, and the snow started to begin to fall about an hour ago. It wasn't even flurries to start with, instead a steady stream of flakes that have left a sheet of white across the fields and ground, along with gusts of wind. Night is fast approaching, so I made it just in time.

Parking, I hop out of the car and look around to see if I spot the dog and quickly walk to the barn, and I look in, only to see Cosmo chewing on some hay. Closing the door, I bundle my coat around my body and make my way to the inn as quickly as possible.

There are no signs of Knox or the dog.

The door to the inn is unlocked, so I let myself in, and it's dark except for the minimal light from outside.

"Knox?" I call out and look around for any indications of where he could be.

I get nothing, and suddenly a fear hits me that he isn't here or that he took the dog somewhere. He did mention that if he found another solution...

Oh no.

"Knox?" Now I panic and begin to search the sitting and dining area to find nothing.

Picking up my pace, I race toward the kitchen.

"Madison?" I hear him say my name as he appears in the doorway to the kitchen. "What are you doing here? I thought you would be back at the end of the weekend?"

"With the storm coming, I decided to come back early." *Or my head is a mess and I needed to see you pronto.* "Where is the dog? Did you get rid of the dog? Really? I leave for forty-eight hours, and you make him disappear?"

He holds his palms up to stop me. "Woman, you really drive me crazy. Am I always the villain? Can you even handle the thought of me being a somewhat decent human?"

I open my mouth, but nothing comes out.

He steps back, inviting me to pass into the illuminated room.

Walking into the kitchen, my eyes immediately dart to my new favorite dog lying on the floor in front of the fire-place near the nook that crackles with heat.

"You kept him!" I can't get to the dog fast enough and lean down to pet his ears as his head perks up.

"Yeah, I'm a giver, so he got to stay."

Glancing back, I see Knox is leaning against a counter and watching me take in the news that I misjudged him.

Assessing the dog, I see he has a blanket, a new collar, and a giant bone to chew on. He is living a good life.

"Where did you get all of this?"

"I went to the pet store this morning."

I stand again to focus my attention on Knox. "But it's the day after Thanksgiving, that's insanity if you go shopping then."

"Perks of being a Blisswood; we get to skip lines, and the pet shop owner owed me a favor."

Looking between the dog and Knox, I'm trying to figure out what's happening. "There is a tag on his collar."

"Yeah, the vet owed me a favor too, and I gave him a bottle of vino to open his office this morning. He checked for a chip. He's a year and half old, and we found the owners, who admitted they were moving out of state and didn't expect him to get so big. He escaped the yard before they had a chance to find him a new home."

My hand finds my heart. "That's horrible."

"It is," he agrees and waits for all the facts to sink in. Knox looks at the floor then back up to me. "He can stay here."

A flood of happiness comes over me at his words. "He grew on you that much?"

Knox plays it cool, but I can see he looks at the dog with fondness. He shrugs a shoulder as the fire brightens our faces. "I mean, this place should have a dog, right? Someone mentioned that once."

A smile tugs on my mouth, as I did say that. "What's his name?"

Knox grins and scratches his cheek as he prepares himself to tell me. His eyes land on me, as he seems to want to watch my reaction. "Pretzel."

I blink a few times at the name. "Bullshit."

"Nope. That is 100% his name according to the old owners."

We both look at Pretzel then back to one another.

This has to be a sign.

"Anything else you want to charge in here and assume I've done?" he asks me with knowing eyes.

"No. I should go." Because my mind is going blank right now.

I turn to leave but don't get far, as he strides a few steps in front of me to block my exit through the door. "Not a fucking chance. The roads right now are a mess."

Trying to avoid his gaze, I attempt to pull his arm away from the closed gate he's created, only for him to grab my wrist in a way that feels like this is our turning point, and he won't let go. "I mean it, Madison, don't debate this. We don't even have power, only the generator in the barn works."

"Oh, so now you dictate when I can and can't go?"

What the hell? Why am I challenging him on this?

He rolls his eyes. "Jesus, you are difficult." His sight lands on me again, and I see that he too is breathing faster than normal. "You can sleep in one of the guest rooms for all I care and freeze there, but at least you're not on the road."

Staring at his mouth and recalling the last five minutes of this man who is anything but selfish, I know I owe him more than my brain short circuiting.

It's time.

Time for my courageous punch to hit him.

"What if I don't want to stay in the guest room?"

Knox snickers. "Really never-ending with you."

He lets my arm go, only for me to reattach us because my hands cup his face, holding him in place.

"What if I slide into your bed whether you invite me or not?" I rasp.

His facial expression doesn't change as he pauses for a

beat, so I step closer to ensure our bodies touch, sliding my arms up around his neck.

"You better be prepared for a long night then." His voice is a gravelly seductive tone.

"Is that a warning?" I wonder.

His eyes land on my mouth. "It's a promise you'll never forget. Because I'll make you shake and tremble until you plead for me to stop by saying my name over and over." A smirk forms, but it doesn't get a chance to stretch far because I'm on my toes to reach up for my lips to seal with his own.

Our sparks fuse and our breaths merge to become two people tangled together.

I think he may be as hungry for this as I am, which is why we don't stop kissing. Every kiss we share is better than the first or second we shared all those weeks ago, and those were already exceptional.

The moment he manages to get my coat off, letting it carelessly fall to the floor, I climb him like a tree, because we are finally going to cross the line.

15

MADISON

My back lands on the mattress of Knox's bed as he hovers over me, our mouths never parting from our fury of kisses.

He has the fireplace on in his room too, which gives us a glow to see what we're doing, but I can't focus as my hands and mouth act on their own accord.

Tugging on his shirt, I come to a sitting position to make it easier, so we only have to part for a second as he discards the shirt up and over his head. Then his powerful kisses lead me back down as his hands pin my wrists to the bed.

Our labored breathing is the soundtrack to our chaotic kisses and bodies tangling.

Knox trails his lips down to my neck where he stops to lick my skin as my entire body arches up into him. My nipples pebble under the fabric, and I feel my skin form goosebumps.

We need to go faster, I'm impatient.

He must sense this, as he lets go of my wrists and his fingers move to fumble with the buttons on my blouse, clearly patience isn't for him either, as both his hands rip the buttons open, and I don't care that it was the last time I wore that blouse—worth it.

"This is what getting stranded with you is like?" My voice is hoarse because I'm sinking underneath him into a frenzy of desire.

His mouth drags down to my breasts that spill out of the cups of my black lace bra, and his eyes peer up. "You have no idea yet." His hand squeezes through the fabric as his lips capture and tease one nipple with the lace between us.

I moan, bite my bottom lip, and hood my eyes closed because everything feels sensitive, and my body is melting under his touch.

My thighs open wide to allow him to settle between my legs and his hard length presses against my center. I'm going dizzy with need.

But my hands seem to understand that we have to move this along, and I begin to unbuckle his belt. He mumbles some unrecognizable sound as he retreats to take over, as we need efficiency right now. I watch him, eyes hazed with desire as he looks at me.

"I need to find a condom. We don't have proof, but statistics seem to show that a lot of unexpected pregnancies happen here at Olive Owl."

It makes me laugh because he isn't even joking. He leans down to give me a quick kiss before he scrambles to the side of the bed, removing his jeans in the process.

I take the opportunity to breathe and control this giddy smile that is taking over me.

But I only get a second before he is back, towering over me until his arms hook under my knees. He pulls me in a swift movement to the end of the mattress before he grabs hold of the waist of my jeans and pulls them down in one go. His antics cause my legs to move up and my ankles to land on his shoulder.

The feeling of his kisses on my calf are tantalizingly slow as he travels up to my inner thighs. "I need you now, Knox," I plead softly as I begin to peel off my panties, meeting him halfway. He finishes the task until I am left in only a bra.

With a smirk, his finger slides along my slit where he feels how incredibly ready for him I am, because I've been waiting for longer than I can admit. "I know, baby."

He opens the little package with the corner of his mouth and lowers his boxers, proving that all my hopes for his size have come true.

"Looks like something matches the size of your ego."

"And you're not complaining."

Watching him sheathe his cock with the condom is so incredibly sexy, and it excites me that he is preparing himself for me; it's the sign that we are doing this.

Then he's over me and I feel him settle between my legs, his length rubbing against my clit, causing me to clench inside in anticipation.

"Please."

He kisses me tenderly. "Ah, you said please," he coos in a playful whisper.

A droll laugh escapes me right before it turns into a gasp because he's slowly traveling deep inside of me.

My toes rest on his ass as my thighs spread wide. I use my nails to hold on for dear life by sinking them into his skin.

"Fuck, you were worth the wait," he groans out as the tip of his cock hits me deep, which makes me close my eyes while he takes over my body.

But he brings me back to reality by capturing my mouth

with his as we begin to sync together. And in this moment, we want it hard and deep, proving that we should have been doing this all along.

Our fingers lace and hold tightly as we both grunt and moan from an impending release that will come soon.

"Don't stop," I murmur against his lips just in case now is the moment that Knox wants to show off his stamina.

His teeth nip at my neck. "I couldn't even if I tried."

My body presses up to bring him deeper and my internal walls wrap tightly around him because I need to feel every inch of him.

With our mouths fusing together, we move, racing toward a finish line because we don't want slow in this moment. We're feral and lost in one another. A few months of back and forth finally combusting.

"This is what you want, shortcake?"

"Now isn't the time for a discussion," I breathe out the words. I hold him tighter against me as he thrusts inside of me.

We both have subtle smirks on our faces when our eyes catch, before we both tilt our centers until we are reaching the point of no return.

A few minutes later, Knox collapses on top of me but careful not to crush me. A sinfully satisfied chuckle comes out as a rumble from the back of his throat.

"I haven't had enough," he warns me.

Before I can ask him to embellish what he means, he's off of me to dispose of the condom, and I lie there completely in a daze of happy endorphins as the wind howls against the glass of the window. But the temporary break is short, because Knox is back with a new condom that he throws onto the mattress.

"Back so soon?" I say as I come up to my propped elbows to study him, naked and in his glory.

"I said I want more." He drops to his knees, coaxes my legs open to station himself, and grips my hips to give him a better view of what he is eyeing.

I purposely let my thighs spread out and my toes dig into the mattress, with my knees up, inviting him to do what he wants with me.

"Bra off," he demands.

I obey and toss it to the side, and I love the way his eyes travel between my breasts that are extra perky today from the cold and the fact they want to be played with.

But they will have to wait, because Knox brings my legs to his shoulders and his mouth lands on my pussy, causing me to near spasm from the touch of his tongue, both from his talent and the fact that I'm still throbbing from our first round.

And the sounds he makes when he laps up my juices should be a crime; he really does enjoy making me go senseless.

"Yes, oh God, yes." My hands claw the sheets because my entire body is on fire.

His hand splays across my stomach to keep me down and in place as he works my clit with circles right after he dips his tongue inside of me.

"I'm addicted to your taste. Your fucking bewitching taste, a potion," he tells me right before he returns to his pursuit that leaves me gasping and moaning in approval.

My fingers comb through his hair to hold onto him between my legs.

"Fuck me, Knox. I want more too," I pant out, voice husky.

I'm wired up, ready, and he knows this because he stops just as I'm about to hit the peak.

His hands land on my obliques, and he guides me to slide up toward the pillows as he kisses up my stomach to move with me.

"I need you on your side. Be compliant, shortcake." He's getting the next condom ready.

I giggle at his urgency but do as he requests.

Where I'm lying on my side, he slides up tightly from behind me, his hand traveling up my front, plucking a nipple, before enclosing around my throat to ensure he can steal all my kisses by guiding my chin back to him.

Kissing him, I feel held captive because he has me, and I don't mind. I'm not sure I've made it clear that I'm giving myself over to him.

Releasing my mouth, he brings my hair to the side, kissing a trail from the back of my neck down my spine, super sensitive and light, yet with the ability to have me tingling at every point of my body. Right before he slides into me from behind, he stills.

"Tell me, did you return to Olive Owl today for the dog or for me?"

Our eyes meet with an intensity that is as powerful as the ability he has to make me feel like I'm floating out of this world.

I can't lie to him when we are in such an intimate position.

"You. It's because of you, Knox."

"Good answer," he simpers as he leads us into our new round of sweaty bodies, longing kisses, and hands interlinking.

"Knox," I whisper his name in a heavenly sounding tone.

I'm getting lost in him. I could be going blind and it wouldn't matter because all my senses are focused on where we are connected together in this very moment.

"You're going to come for me again," he mutters against my lips, already a reader of my body, because there is a reason he said that right now.

I nod as the stimulation against my clit is too much, and I begin to tremble in his hold, spasming around his cock inside of me.

"Knox," I nearly scream out, but he holds my jaw in place to ensure our gaze doesn't break.

"I've got you, Madison. Let go."

I do, and I lose myself completely in the feeling of freefalling.

"Good girl, just like that," he whispers as he grunts from the feeling his cock must be experiencing as I shake around him, tightening from my orgasm, and with a few more movements he too stills then rides the wave with me.

It takes a few moments for us to register that we both just came again. Holding me there on his bed, we are completely in a trance, considering how much sex we just had in the span of probably thirty minutes.

"We are animals," I comment with a heavy breath.

"We're not even halfway through the night." He collapses back on the mattress, and I smile at his face that shows me he is clearly relaxed and content.

When I roll into his arms, he opens one eye to peek at me. "You're not going to the guest room then?"

"Nah, I would rather freeze in a bed with you." I pretend it's an inconvenience.

"I'll make sure you stay perfectly warm but only if you listen and obey," he teases me.

My fingers crawl up his chest. "Hmm, let me think about that…"

"You have two minutes. I need to go take care of this." He points to the second condom we've used.

"Okay, maybe I'll be here when you get back," I taunt.

But I have no plans of going anywhere tonight.

Instead, I get comfortable under the blankets and rest my head on the pillow. He returns from the bathroom a minute later, and I can't stop admiring his body, his lean muscles, his tattoo in full view, or his eyes that have a glimmering sheen.

"Not a bad view," I lament as I pull the sheet up to cover myself.

"Likewise." He grabs a few items from his dresser then throws them to me—a shirt and sweatpants. "As much as I plan on keeping you warm tonight, the heating is off due to the storm, and it's supposed to get to minus temperatures tonight."

"Thanks. I have my weekend bag in the car, but I like this option better," I admit as he slides under the covers to join me in bed.

Lying on his side, he rests his head against a propped elbow. "I prefer you naked."

"Well, it's good that I'm not cold yet then." I set the clothes to the side and shuffle my body to sink deeper into the mattress. My fingertips want to explore, and I begin to trace lines on his body.

Knox in turn rests his hand on my hip and then we lie there with eyes glued to one another.

"Stuck in a snowstorm with you, sharing a bed… there are worse things." I smirk at him as I continue to enjoy feeling every curve of his body.

His fingers move to brush hair behind my ear. "What would you have done if I wasn't adamant you stay?"

I shimmy closer to him and hook a leg over his body. "Probably walk to the door and then realize I can't take it anymore and still stay." I place a gentle kiss on his inner arm.

His response is to pull me flush to his body and roll me so I'm lying on top of him, resting my chin on his chest.

"Madison, don't ever make me wait again."

"I thought you said you wait for no one." I kiss his pec then drag my lips over his skin for a feathery touch.

I realize that I can't get enough of feeling his body, inhaling his scent that smells of firewood, or tasting the saltiness of sweat on his skin.

"You aren't no one."

Knox dips his head down to capture my mouth, and I can only smile as he kisses me. I have no idea what he means, but it sounds promising.

I wrap my arms and legs around him to drag him with me as I roll to my back, because I like him on top of me, and I also get a thrill from countering his previous move.

There is something sexy about a man shifting his weight to one side, which naturally causes his muscles to flex and his eyes to stare down on you.

"So," I drag out, "here we are."

"Let's talk about it tomorrow. Right now, we have one priority and that is to stay warm. Hot, even." He begins to nuzzle his nose into my neck. This man is insatiable, needs no recovery time.

And quite frankly, I enjoy reaching between us to take hold of his length.

"Let me do my part, you know, to ensure we don't get

cold." My sultry voices turns on as I stroke him, the act turning me on.

He curses a moan under his breath as I continue with my rhythm, feeling his fingers slide between my legs.

"You're definitely contributing."

My leg wraps around his waist, using my strength to pull him down on me. His cock settling between my folds and tempting us both.

But then we stop, and a flicker of sincerity comes over us. Our lips meet for a kiss. Our foreheads touch and we lie there in an embrace, touching one another, but we slow down.

We're going to savor every moment of tonight.

"When morning comes, tell me this doesn't change things," I whisper my request as we continue our soft caresses.

He kisses the curve of my shoulder. "It changes everything, Madison, and I think that's exactly what you want."

I don't answer because the man who was my disdain for months is actually right.

16

KNOX

Waking, I instantly feel Madison in my arms. Somewhere between round four and five—or was it six—we fell asleep.

The last few days have been unexpected, from becoming a dog owner to Madison showing up, only for us to finally, after months of circles, land in bed together. And she's better than every fantasy combined.

A mixture of her cotton candy smell and the laundry detergent of my clothes hits my nose. I would rather she were naked, but I know the moment I pull back the duvet that a sharp cold will hit us, as the fire burned out hours ago.

Instead, we have relied on good old-fashioned body heat to keep us warm.

She stirs in my hold as she slowly wakes. I watch her blink her eyes a few times before she has a drowsy smile form on her face, as she must be recalling last night and the early morning hours in her head.

We both mumble and stretch slightly, but don't break our embrace.

"Knox." Her sleepy voice still manages to wrap my name playfully around the room, as if my name is her greeting. She's in a good mood from what I can hear.

"Shortcake," I return in the same tone.

She lifts the sheet slightly to glance down then up.

"It's morning, I can't help it if I wake up hyped and ready."

"I think I know something that may help." She flashes me a mischievous look before slithering down my body and disappearing under the sheet.

Best morning ever.

I can't even deter her, not that I would try.

Her mouth lands on the head of my cock and the sounds she makes indicate that this may be her favorite way to wake me up.

The swirl of her tongue along my dick has me no longer able to think about the morning ahead. I'm getting mouth-fucked by a blonde-haired beauty who is wearing my college shirt, and if I were to stick my hand down the cotton pants she's wearing then I know she would be ready for me too.

This is what men dream about, and it's my reality.

I hiss out a breath as she takes me deeper, sucking harder, and treating me like her breakfast.

But as much as me coming down her throat is a brilliant way to start the day, I need her wrapped around my cock.

Reaching for a condom on the side table, I make a mental note that it's the last one from this box. I lift up the sheet and bring the condom down to her view, but she grabs it and throws it to the side. Her focus is on getting me off, and my brain is struggling to comprehend how magnificent she is.

Her hand presses up against my chest to ensure that I

don't disrupt her efforts. And it may be the sweetest thing I've done while having a woman go down on me but I hold her hand by entwining our fingers while my other hand strokes her hair as she continues to drag her tongue from my base to tip.

I groan and close my eyes. "Madison, I'm getting there," I warn her as my muscles tighten and warmth spreads below my navel.

Her eyes look up for approval, and I grin a confirmation flooded with adoration.

Then I let go, jets of my come landing in her mouth that she licks and swallows, moans even.

I may black out. I need a minute to digest that the woman in my bed gets better by the hour. My heart beats on full speed as Madison returns to lie against my chest.

"Good morning."

"It's... it's a great morning." I blow out a breath. "Give me a moment, I need you to come."

Her finger shushes my mouth. "I'm already satisfied, and you probably need your strength for later."

"Such a caring soul." My arm wraps around her as we lie there. "I'll leave in a minute to get more wood for the *fire* and let Pretzel out."

"I can't believe you're keeping him." She can't hide her gushing praise, and I'm happy about that.

"Well, he's pretty chill. I brought him for Thanksgiving at my brother's, and by end of dinner, we figured out that everyone at some point had given Pretzel bits of food since he charmed his way around the table. My niece and nephew are infatuated with him too. I mean, maybe I should have a companion here, since Bennett and Grayson don't live here anymore."

She laughs as she rests her chin on her hand that's on

my chest. "You're going to become one of those dog people, I can see it. And… I'm relieved he's with you. I didn't really like the idea of making him find somewhere else to live. Pretzel is my favorite breed, I'm jealous a little."

"You can see him whenever you want, you just have to see me too for that to happen," I tease her, but deep down I want to keep double-checking on what *is* going on between us. I'm not used to this situation. After all, she waited far longer than I would have liked. In fact, she set world records for holding out on me.

"I think I can live with that," she assures me, and I'm comforted, as all signs are encouraging. "It's nice that you are so close with your family, lucky too. I can imagine family dinners are entertaining."

I scoff from the mere thought. "More than." Especially if I bring a date to the table; they've all been waiting years for that to happen. They think I can't be tamed, but they're wrong. And although it never crossed my mind with other women, with Madison, it very much flashes in my head what introducing her as my date would entail.

"It looks like a complete whiteout. When do you think the roads will be clear?" She looks across the room out the window. I forgot to close the black-out curtain—I was a little occupied.

"Hard to say, as it's a holiday weekend. I think the snow stopped, so it should only be flurries."

Madison moves to straddle me and she's an angelic vision. "Those flurries can be dangerous. Guess to be extra safe then, I should stay here with you." Her fingers walk up from my navel to my heart.

A simple fact dawns on me as I grip her middle. "You struggle to say what you're really thinking, I mean when it involves you and me. Tell me what you want, right now, for today."

Her upper lip ticks as if she understands what I mean. "Okay. I want to stay here with you—in bed, not in bed. While you go do manly things like shovel snow or collect wood, I'll make you breakfast. And at breakfast you can tell me about your dad or growing up here at the winery. Then after breakfast, we will keep warm together. That's what I want."

I bring my upper body up to kiss her mouth because her answer is perfect. I tuck her hair behind her shoulders as I mumble into our kiss, "Then that is what you shall get."

———

RETURNING to the kitchen after going outside, I stomp snow off my boots on the mat by the back door as Pretzel shakes off snow, getting it all over the kitchen floor, and jumps straight to the spot by the fire that I feel like is now his territory.

The ten minutes of hellish cold and a few gusts of wind and snow was completely worth it, as the warmth from the fire is a welcome temperature change.

But the real reward is the view of Madison in my sweatshirt and pants behind the gas stove that luckily works despite lack of electricity. She's stirring a pot and seems to have been humming as she pours ingredients in.

"Turkish coffee?" she offers. "I made some on the stove since you had cardamon on the spice rack."

Removing all my outerwear, I feel the corner of my mouth tug at this scene. "Sounds perfect. What other magic do you have brewing there?"

I walk slowly to her and notice the way she smiles at

her creation that she's stirring with a wooden spoon. My arm encircles around her waist from behind and I kiss the spot below her ear.

"Pancakes would have been too predictable, and oatmeal is perfect for a snowy day. I added some brown sugar, nuts, raisins, chia seeds, and banana. We need to replenish all those lost calories." She sways in my arms, and I run my lips along the base of her throat.

"That we do. You're an oatmeal eater?"

"Yeah, you?"

I hum a sound, as truthfully it feels surreal to have her in the kitchen of Olive Owl and preparing oatmeal. "Actually, my dad was really into it. Swore it was a man's meal and ate it until the very end," I reflect. "I just realized that I haven't had any since he passed."

She turns in my arms with an affectionate look and loops her arms around my neck. "I can whip something else up if you don't want to—"

"Nah, actually I think oatmeal sounds good."

Funny how little things come to light. Was me avoiding a certain breakfast item a way of mourning? And it's Madison who makes me bring it back into my life without thought.

She stretches across to pour coffee and then hands me a mug. "You miss him?"

"It was expected, his departure, and we prepared for it. Do I miss playing poker or discussing Olive Owl over bottles of wine with him? Sometimes, but it's been almost two years. And a lot has happened in two years."

Because of our dad's passing, Grayson came back, Bennett became a dad, and Lucy buries herself in school. The reins of Olive Owl have been handed over to us, and I intend to keep it to a high standard, even if I have to be the one who lives here 24/7.

I take a sip of the drink. "Mmm, that's good."

"Did your mom cook breakfast a lot?"

"You're full of questions. I guess... I don't really remember. Waffles ring a bell. With Lucy, we really got into those cinnamon rolls from the grocery store. Helen also whips up some eggs and bacon when she's on duty."

Madison smiles wide. "Ah yes, Helen." She flashes her eyes at me. "By any chance did she partner us up with a hidden agenda?"

No hesitation in my mind. "Absolutely." I set my mug on the counter and pull Madison tightly into my body before lifting her up and planting her on the counter near the stove. "She'll bring you pie when she finds out," I warn her with a grin.

"Will she? What happens when this weekend ends?" She's searching my eyes for a clue.

I don't have a clear answer, only that this shouldn't be a one-time thing. "You don't want this to be only a week-end," I remind her of what her brain must be telling her.

"You don't do relationships," she counters, with her head cocking to the side.

My finger taps the tip of her nose. "That's an assumption."

"You avoid them. I've heard your history in the teacher's lounge."

I scoff at her explanation. "Hey, it's true that I haven't been in a long-term relationship in, well... a while. There hasn't been someone worth romantic dinners or discussions about shared calendars or debating who will stop at the grocery store for missing ingredients for dinner."

She lowers her head as she struggles to keep her smile under wraps. "A shared calendar sounds like misery. Tell me about this woman who spent the night." She's playing coy.

"She's intriguing enough," I tell her. "Maybe even exhilarating. Definitely need more time to figure out what to do with her."

"I mean, I also need to see if you are bearable beyond this weekend," she deadpans then gives me an I-love-to-tease-you look.

"You know I have a few ways to persuade you," I warn her.

"I will be the judge of that." She articulates the T. "Anyway, I'm not sure how we do this."

My hands come to cradle her face between my palms. "I don't know. I've never... you're different." I'm not exactly going to advertise that I've never had a serious relationship or that I want to treat her differently to any other conquest. I want to be everything that I've never been to a woman, but I'm not ready to admit that.

"I'm not afraid to challenge you, that's a change for you. Not exactly earth-shattering."

I want to tell her that it's more than that. It's the way she fits around my body, or her ability to make me angry but want her desperately at the same time, her beautiful smile that makes me feel at ease. This undeniable feeling inside of me that I'm heading into my own corner of the world and she's coming with.

The back of her knuckles glide along my short stubble. "I just mean that if we are just playing around then I think it's better we do so privately, and if it's something else... well, Lucy is my student, and I've never done *this* with a relative of my student."

"Oh, really? I thought you would be a pro at this," I sarcastically joke with her.

"Ha-ha. And what about your family? Something tells me that I would need like a whole tutorial on how to deal with them."

She isn't wrong there.

Leaning forward, I kiss her. A simple kiss to bring us back to coffee and oatmeal.

"Should we focus on breakfast?" I suggest.

"I mean, I already had my protein fix for the day, but yeah, oatmeal sounds delicious," she quips, and I love her devilish grin—no, I love her ability to think dirty like me.

Madison hops off the counter and grabs two bowls, and then I see her slide the dog bowl off the counter by the kitchen sink.

"Pretzel is not eating oatmeal," I state firmly.

"I know." She shows me the bowl and I see the beast gets his own gourmet meal of wet dog food, some peanut butter, and a small bacon dog treat on top.

"You're going to use me for access to Pretzel, aren't you?"

She squeezes my cheek. "You'll never know," she jokes with a wink.

"Here I was thinking it's my ability to make you come."

"That's just a bonus, babe," she mundanely says as she sets the dish in front of a happy Pretzel who is wagging his tail.

During breakfast, we talk about her time on her aunt and uncle's farm growing up or how her addiction to chocolate-covered pretzels goes even further because back in the city she would go to this shop that had different flavors, with sprinkles. She gets excited like a kid when she talks about it. I tell her about my boxing routine with Drew and the shit I got up to with my brothers growing up.

Every smile and sip of coffee as she sits across from me feels like she's rooting down into my life. She would fit into my days, always has. Madison is the opposite of every woman that I've been with, down to her understanding when I speak in agricultural language.

After placing the dishes in the sink, I notice her shoulders drop low, and she lets out an audible breath. "The guests that were supposed to come canceled?"

"Yeah, they didn't want to travel in this weather, which is understandable. Drew should be stopping by later if he shovels himself out of his driveway. But I could just text him that all is good here…" It trails off as I scratch the back of my neck.

"Is it good, Knox?" she challenges with a raspy voice and brow raised as she throws the tea towel to the side.

She's tantalizing me, encouraging me to lead us into an afternoon filled with sex.

"I would say so. I mean, I think we have some discovering to do." I slowly stride to her before landing my hands on her ass, causing her to gasp.

"Let's go get warm," she suggests.

I invite her to jump up into my arms so I can carry her as her legs wrap around me. "Great idea, but let's see if we can find another box of condoms first."

She playfully pushes my shoulder. "How do you not have a larger supply?"

"Because despite what you think, I don't spend weekends with a woman in my bed," I shoot back.

"Oh?" Her voice and head perk up.

My eyes widen to show that she shouldn't doubt me, and then her lips quirk out before a soft smile erupts.

"Why do I feel so pulled to you?" she whispers as she drags her mouth down my neck.

"Because we have a spark."

By the time I drop her onto my bed, I realize the sad truth that we are out of essential props, and we still have another night ahead of us. "Shit," I curse under my breath.

"What?" She looks at me, concerned.

"Looks like I am doing everything to you except burying my cock deep inside of you." I deflate. I mean, it's not a bad way to spend a Saturday night, with my tongue and fingers worshipping her body, but my dick inside of her would be by far more phenomenal.

She pulls me on top of her, taking hold of my face as her legs lock around me to bring me to her body. "I'm on the pill. Assuming you haven't done any small-town swinging lately or dates at Rooster Sin then…"

Am I walking on water? Is this happening?

"I'm completely safe. In fact…" I chortle a laugh that I'm about to admit this. "I haven't been with anyone since before I saved your pretzels, and I'm all checked out."

"Really?" Again, I surprise her.

"Honestly."

She kisses me quickly. "Only book boyfriends for me, and they are fictional, so they don't count. Now those statistics on conception and unplanned pregnancy at Olive Owl you mentioned…"

"My brothers being total idiots with birth control… I think." My face must make a cartoonish look before I slam my lips down onto her own.

"*I think* works for me. Now get inside of me," she urges because we both need this.

Trust is big, and that deserves a union that involves so many *ohs*.

The moment we both manage to get naked from the waist down and I'm about to enter her, I stop. "Are you sure?"

"Yes. I want to feel you like this." Her eyes have a glint of vulnerability, and I'm falling even faster off a mountain that I didn't even know I climbed… with her.

"The thing is… I've never done it bareback, and I have a feeling that I might get so addicted to you that I will never want anything else."

My eyes indicate for her to think about it, what I'm saying. It's her call if she lets me in, because this means more than just a weekend fueled by passion. It means something more longstanding, and even I can admit that.

"I'll take that risk." A wry smile forms on her mouth.

I kiss her and then it begins.

The internal confirmation that I don't want anyone else. Because I think we are the goddamn dynamite that I've been waiting to explode to make me really appreciate life.

And damn, what do I do with something like that?

17

MADISON

I smile as my finger circles the top of the glass of cola as I sit in Rooster Sin. Ellie and I decided the staff meeting was enough to send us here to stuff our faces with hot wings to the sounds of bad karaoke.

"When the spaceship lands and asks for volunteers then I'm sure you will step forward, eager and ready." Ellie looks at me to see if I'm listening.

"Yeah, aliens, sure," I mumble and take a sip from my straw.

She nudges my arm and grins like a Cheshire cat. "So you do kind of listen. I wasn't sure, as your head has been in the clouds all night."

Breaking my daydreaming spell of repeating scenes from the weekend, I shake my head. "Sorry, I guess my mind is somewhere else."

"We know it wasn't in early-morning detention duty, so does it have everything to do with a certain man who goes by the name of Knox?"

I blush, I absolutely blush.

"Maybe."

"A whole weekend, huh?" She looks off into the distance, trying to imagine the fantasy.

A lazy smile spreads on my lips from the information I shared with her in the teachers' lounge the other morning.

"What's next? Going there tonight for a little action or waiting for him to whisk you away for a romantic dinner?" She drinks from her bottle of beer.

My lips slide side to side as I ponder, but really, I am digesting the fact that it wasn't a one-time thing. "Going with the flow," I admit.

I left Olive Owl Sunday afternoon, and my body has been recovering since. I'm surprised we didn't break his bed, and I didn't know it was possible to enjoy the feeling of being sore from being thoroughly worshipped.

When he walked me to my car, he kissed me goodbye, promising me that there was more to come. We've texted a bit, but it's a busy time with both of our jobs. Nonetheless, he doesn't leave my thoughts. Not even Braden Plums could piss me off in twelfth-grade English class, and normally that kid is a thorn.

"That's really good, Madison," she tells me with a softness that is purely genuine. "Things are falling into place for you here in Bluetop."

They are.

We both look at Rooster Sin's small stage and cringe. "They are awful." I'm referring to the fire department trying to belt out a rendition of Guns N' Roses' "Paradise City."

"Yeah, well, let them have their fun. It must suck hoping to put out fires, only to save cats from trees or run the annual car wash for charity."

I laugh at her statement then notice her eyes directed behind me.

"Wow, someone is claiming you with a mere glance. Wish my husband would have a broody grin like that," she quips then widens her eyes.

Instantly, I turn around on the stool to see Knox entering the bar with a sly grin and Drew by his side. I wasn't planning on seeing him, nor did I mention that I would be here.

Both men approach us, and while Drew scans the room, Knox makes it clear that I'm his destination.

"Madison." His eyes are glued to me as he strolls to the free spot next to me. My glance shoots up to his sinful mouth that may just convince me to run away from here, and now.

"Knox," I breathe out.

"A beer?" Drew asks him then directs his attention to the bar.

"Sure, what are you ladies having?" Knox asks Ellie and me.

Ellie chuckles softly under her breath. "I'm having a 0% beer, and my guess is Madison here is having a flashback." She clucks her tongue right before I nudge her with my elbow.

"What brings you two to Rooster Sin?" I ask as Knox's and my eyes stay fixed on one another, even when Drew hands him a beer.

"Thought we would grab a drink, as we just had a gym session. You?"

I feel heat flushing my face from having him near. "We had a staff meeting earlier so thought we would unwind."

"Hmm," Drew murmurs. "Didn't want to use your and Knox's other method of unwinding?" He throws me a knowing grin before tipping his beer bottle back to take a drink.

My mouth gapes open slightly from his sentence. Knox just laughs awkwardly. "Drew noticed a few changes at Olive Owl the other day."

"Yep. A dog, for one. Two bowls of leftover food, two wine glasses, two plates, a random bra—"

Knox plants his hand against Drew's chest. "Such an observer you are."

Let me die now… in Knox's bed, preferably.

"I think I'm going to head to the little ladies' room," I say as I slide off my stool with a tight smile plastered across my face.

It doesn't take long for me to hightail it to the bathroom, only when I turn to close the door to the little room behind me, Knox is there, and he steps in then slams the door shut and swings me around until my back hits the door. He does it so fast that I have no chance to understand what is happening.

His hands travel up my sides, and I can't even hide my approval to this moment between us, which is why I offer him my mouth to kiss me.

We kiss like two people drunk on lust because our hands wander, and we try to kiss harder, as if we could get more in this moment.

"I guess we are not forgetting about last weekend," I grit out a teasing remark that causes him to grumble against the skin of my neck.

"I want you right now."

I snort a laugh as he continues to explore down my cleavage with his mouth. "Knox, you're crazy. We are not going to do it here."

"I know, but tell that to my hands or my mouth that wants to suck your juices. And my dick—well, he just never listens." His mouth kisses a trail back up and along my jawline.

My arms encircle his neck. "You are making this really hard," I breathe before I bite my bottom lip from the pure torture he is creating when he brushes his lips against the lobe of my ear, his breath cascading down my skin. He steps closer to me, pressing our bodies tightly together, and I feel his cock against my stomach. "Okay, something may be harder," I rasp.

My hands can't stay put and run along his body, anywhere I can touch.

"Why was my bra lying around Olive Owl?"

Knox pauses and looks at me like I am an idiot for asking. "Remember, you lost it on the way back to your car?"

"You mean when we did it on the stairs? True." I frown.

We continue to kiss like two teenagers making out.

"Thanks for the text," I say in an attempt to bring us normal conversation. He sent me an adorable photo of Pretzel lying on his bed then told me to have a good day. "How were invoices?"

"Boring." His kisses run along my collarbone. "How were seventh-period seniors?"

Right, because we actually talk via text about things not orgasm-related.

"I think okay. I mean, I may have forgotten to give them homework."

What the hell? We are having a casual conversation while our bodies run wild.

"Your panties. Give them to me," he instructs me, and I look at him, puzzled.

Oh, there goes our normal conversation out the window.

But he is already moving down my body, taking my leggings and panties with. Lucky for him I'm in flats.

"Do I even want to know what you have planned?" I can't help the droll smile forming on my lips as I watch him inhale the scent of the damp cloth, groan in satisfaction, then tuck the cloth into his back pocket before helping redress me, kissing a trail up my legs.

"Don't question a starving man," he pleads with a pout before returning to standing.

When our eyes meet, we slow, we simmer, we touch and have giddy looks.

"Everyone out there will know what we're up to," I state.

He brushes a few strands of my hair behind my ear. "Who cares?"

My mouth twitches from a smile that wants to form.

"What if I want everyone to know that you're mine?" He seems to be surprised that he just said that, yet a confident look rests on his face.

Holy smokes, my pelvic floor muscles are discovering a new way to clench for survival.

I pretend to be unaffected, but struggle. "We're new."

"Nah, we've been circling one another for a while."

My fingers play with the fabric of his shirt against his chest. "We'll get there."

He leans down to kiss me tenderly, claiming me the way he does.

After pulling away, he tilts his head to the door behind me. "We should get out of here—I mean this bathroom. I know you have to be at school early, and I need to drive to Chicago tomorrow for the day."

"Oh, the joys of adulthood." I sigh.

We both straighten our clothes, but nothing will fix the

fact that I look like a woman completely under the spell of lust and in possession of a softening heart. All because of this man who has made my head spin more times than I can count.

Which is all the more reason that a few days later, when I return from the gym and find Knox waiting outside my apartment leaning against his truck, I know that my world is about to go upside down yet again.

MADISON

I look at Knox with curiosity as I get out of my car on this early evening. He watches me stride toward him from where he's leaning against the door of his car.

"To what do I owe this pleasure, Mr. Blisswood?" I grin and walk into his more-than-welcoming arms.

"I have a surprise for you."

"Oh yeah?" I hear myself purr.

Leaning to the side, he grabs the white box with a bow sitting on the hood of his car then hands it to me.

I look at the box then back to him, with a smile spreading. After a tug of the bow, I open the box, only to squeal in delight.

"You just made my year," I declare as I stare down at the contents of the box.

"Wait, it wasn't one of the many orgasms I delivered?" he feigns doubt.

I give him a sensual look before melding our lips together for a kiss. "This is a tie-breaker," I say against his mouth.

My tongue licks my lips as I stare at the thick pretzel

sticks covered in chocolate and various sprinkles. A few have peanut butter too.

"Got them yesterday when I was in the suburbs for work. Saw them at the bakery near a restaurant we work with."

And he thought of me.

"I love it. Want to watch something with me and get your mind blown by sweet-and-salty snacks?"

Knox pulls me flush to him. "Deal. Pretzel can visit for a few hours, right?" He motions to the back seat of his truck, and I didn't even notice our canine companion sitting at attention, which is hard to ignore, but Knox has me captivated.

Waving a hand, I blow off any rules. "The apartment association can go kiss it." Then I smile at Pretzel who lets out a tiny woof. I hand Knox the box and open the door to let our giant furball out.

A few minutes later we are inside my apartment with Pretzel settled on the floor near the sofa.

"Okay, I need a quick shower."

Knox takes that as an invitation and begins to raise his shirt.

"Whoa there, cowboy. Let me have a real shower," I insist, and he drops his shirt back.

"Fine, but only because I'm going to order some pizza and pick out a series for us to watch."

I point a finger at him. "Ozark? A win-win, you get to watch the action of a drug dealer and I get to stare at Jason Bateman."

"Whoa. That's an assumption that I will let you choose... but you have good taste." He drops the remote to show me that I've won.

A quick shower and I'm toweling off in my bathroom,

debating if I go all in on this chill evening about to happen. I decide that fluffy socks and a long t-shirt with leggings it is.

I laugh when I see him comfortable on my couch, drinking cola from a mug that says *hockey player, billionaire, cowboy #bookboyfriends*.

"Comfortable?" I ask as I shuffle my body onto the sofa next to him.

"Very. You were in the shower that I wasn't allowed to disrupt, so I picked the pizza. Cheese, chicken, pineapple, onions, corn, and BBQ sauce."

"Wow. That's… interesting. Maybe kind of delicious, I don't know. Moment of truth, did you order garlic bread?"

He scoffs at me. "I'm not a rookie."

I smile in response. "How was your wine delivery today?" I sink back into the sofa and Pretzel comes to rest his head on my lap.

"Good. I have to go to Chicago next weekend… You should come with me. We can make a day of it. A friend owns a few restaurants there, so I can get us good reservations." He also pets the dog.

We both seem to ignore the fact that we are heading into dating territory.

I think about his offer, and it does sound fun. "I haven't really been back since I moved. I guess I could do a little shopping and then have a maybe enjoyable lunch with some guy I used to loathe." I move and swing my legs over Knox to straddle him.

"So that's a 'yes, Knox, I'll go with you'?"

"Yep."

"You really didn't plan on heading back? I mean, you must have friends and family there."

My lips quirk out. "Well, friends are busy getting

engaged or moving to Austin or Florida because apparently that's the place to be these days. And I really am estranged from my parents. I'm okay with it all. I wanted to make my own life somewhere, and besides, it's kind of nice being in a place where there's really only one place for coffee, makes decision-making less complicated."

"Alright, you sound confident in your answer. Next Saturday, you and me, all day it shall be." He interlaces our fingers and rests them between us. "By the way, Helen was at Olive Owl the other day helping with holiday decorations and she asked if I had spoken to you lately. Even had a twinkle in her eye."

"What did you say?"

"That I fucked you right where she was standing." My face drops and then a smug look spreads on his face. "Nah, I said that I hadn't seen you in a while other than when you delivered a stray dog to me. She suggested I ask you to come to the Blisswood holiday party, and then she handed me mistletoe to hang because she is *super* subtle."

"Funny. Ran into her at the gym as she finished power-walking around the indoor track, and she said that you are trouble but worth further investigation."

Knox shrugs. "What can I say, words of the wise."

There is a moment of quiet, and I take this opportunity to ask a question that has been nagging at me. Clearing my throat, I look at Knox with inquisition. "Uhm, so Drew obviously knows about you and me." I motion with my finger between us. "Your brothers?" My voice hitches slightly.

Knox seems to take enjoyment from my discomfort at this conversation. "They are smart guys... some of the time. They also have nosy wives, so yeah, they all have an idea. Lucy seems to be in her own world these days."

"Yeah." I scratch the top of my head. "She hasn't looked at me any differently in class, and I'm doing my best not to associate the fact that she is the sister of a certain talented guy who might be wrapping me around his finger."

He kisses the top of my hand that he's holding, a kiss that is all parts sweet. "It's almost winter break, so you're good."

"True," I reflect. It buys me time, but I will eventually have to figure out what to tell Principal Beal should this thing between Knox and me go further. For now, I brush it to the back of my head.

After the pizza arrived, we ate and then watched two episodes of Ozark. I fed Knox chocolate pretzels and got him addicted, as we fought over the peanut-butter-filled ones.

Everything just feels easy, relaxing even, and I like that it feels natural between us.

And okay, we had a quickie session on my couch before he carried me to bed and tucked me in.

Tucked me in!

Pretzel needed to go out, plus Knox needed to get back to Olive Owl, but he fluffed my pillows and snuggled the blanket over my body, before kissing me goodnight again and again.

When he turned to leave, I grabbed his wrist to stop him.

"I had a good night, Knox. I thought it would be odd having a night not driven by passion because then it means we are only that. But tonight felt completely right, and even though I wish you could stay, I still feel like it's a perfect ending."

"Believe it or not, this is new to me, uncharted territory

even. But maybe we're only getting started." He kisses me one long I-hate-to-leave-you kiss and leaves me to sleep well.

———

A WEEK LATER, I walk with a sway toward where Knox is waiting for me, sitting at a table. Jupiter is the name of the restaurant, and it's beautiful. A view over the Chicago River and plates of food with an artistic flair set the scene of this modern yet industrial-feeling venue.

While Knox handled some paperwork and orders with the restaurant owner, I did a little shopping.

Knox's eyes dart down to the little bag in my hands as he stands to pull my chair out. "Do some meandering?"

"Uh-huh."

Once I sit down, he helps slide my chair back under the table and leans down to whisper in my ear, "At the place we discussed in great detail during the car ride here after you told me your fantasy of being tied up and submissive?"

My cheeks feel warm and must be a shade of red. I'm surprised I admitted that on our conversation over, but he seems like someone up to the task. "I may have," I taunt, and I swear that I can hear him growl lowly.

The car ride into the city was a constant discovery of likes and dislikes that we are discovering about one another. And yes, the discussion of lingerie popped into our early-morning coffee-infused drive.

A lace bodysuit called my name when I went shopping and he handled business.

Settling into my seat and taking in my surroundings of the beautifully set table, down to the chic wine glasses, I think my favorite part is Knox sitting across from me in a white button-down shirt and his eyes extra sparkly today as he looks at me.

We are going to have lunch and then do a little walk. He wants to pick up some Christmas gifts for his brothers' kids and then we will head back. It's a bit crowded, as it's weekend and December.

"We get a special menu. Wes who owns the place wants us to try a few things. He and his wife married at Olive Owl, actually," Knox explains.

I take a sip from my water. "Oh? Is he the one who had that wedding that ended up on some blog and made Olive Owl famous?" I heard about it because one of the teachers said I should get my hair done at Bennett's wife's place, as her styling landed on a blog due to a wedding at Olive Owl.

Knox laughs. "We were doing well before that, but yeah, when one of Chicago's leading restaurant entrepreneurs marries at Olive Owl, then it's a nice boost. His friends also come to Olive Owl often for wine tastings, and of course some of our products are here on the menu."

"Sounds perfect. You checked in on Pretzel?"

Knox laughs because we dropped Pretzel off at Grayson's on our way out of town. I stayed in the car, but I heard a five-year-old squeal in excitement. "I got a text that Rosie is insisting he takes part in a tea party and is now begging her parents for a puppy instead of a pony."

"I guess that is a more realistic demand than a pony." I shrug.

I admire the brick of the walls and then my eyes land on the waiter delivering a few plates of food to our table. An array of salads, meats, and roasted vegetables. The waiter explains the sampling, and the moment I bite into the roasted parsnips with a sauce, I think I moan.

"This is… wow, incredible." I slowly savor my bite and

stare at the half lemon on the plate that lies there for decoration. "For the longest time, I wanted to tattoo a lemon to
my lower back."

Knox drops his fork and coughs a laugh. "What?"

"Yeah, I thought it would be kind of cool to have a
lemon on the back of my neck because, you know, life
gives you lemons." My head bounces back and forth as I
take a sip of my iced tea. "But then I realized it would be
better to find something teacher-related. Yet I still have no
tattoos, I keep chickening out."

"Ms. Prim and Proper wants a tattoo. We can do that
one day."

I give him a look that I'm not impressed with the old
title he gave me. "Oh, I know you would help. Sadly, I need
to be drunk and probably in Vegas at some Elvis wedding
to even consider."

Knox cuts into his steak. "Okay, fair enough. What
other secrets are you keeping from me?"

"That wasn't a secret. It was a fact you hadn't yet
discovered. And hmm…" I bring my finger to my mouth to
consider. "I think that's it. What about you, what do you
want? More tattoos? A wife with ten kids? To go into the
pig business?"

"No pigs. Cosmo, chickens, and Pretzel are enough. For
sure another tattoo, not sure what. And eventually a wife,
and if she's hot enough, then sure, we can try for a kid."

I throw a piece of bread at him. "Funny."

"I actually got ordained to marry people at Olive Owl."

My hand slams onto the table. "No way!"

He nods sheepishly with a half-smile.

"Wow, didn't see that coming. Ah, so you deep down
always had a thing for true romance."

He rolls his eyes. "I was never against romance, just

never put it into practice in my personal life," he corrects me.

"Well, good thing something changed." I reach over to squeeze his hand on the table, and his eyes dart down to look at our bodies connected.

We both work on our plates of food and continue to talk about anything that comes to mind. Every laugh feels like our discovery phase is now history. This thing between us is quickly morphing into more than anything I expected.

"Can I ask something?" I play with the amazing dessert inspired by smores on my plate.

"You will anyway," he assures me.

"Grayson mentioned once that you never like to sit under the tree. The one where you forced me to have a planning date, next to the swing. Why did it feel like you didn't mind at all?"

Knox sinks back against the seat, and his look is half like he's been discovered and half vulnerable. "I can't explain it. It just felt like I was meant to try and win you over, and I was inclined to do it there. That spot always reminds me of my mom, but in that moment, I only saw you." I reach across the table to lace our fingers together. "Even when you pretended to be irritated by me, I saw a flicker of someone who was intrigued and enjoys every treacherous second with me."

"You're right."

Our eyes meet and I give him a warm look.

"You and me. We can be something good. Something really good," he tells me, and I feel like he isn't wrong.

"I think so too," I reply.

The rest of our day is constant handholding, dirty jokes, and me easing him from his frustration that the line for pick-up at the doll store isn't shorter. But he promised

Grayson that we would collect Rosie's Christmas gift, so we stay put.

By the time we made it back to Olive Owl it was eight in the evening. We had discussed staying in the city overnight, but I ditched that idea because I like the idea of waking up in Knox's bed and cooking fresh farm eggs. Olive Owl is more appealing to me than any swanky hotel on Michigan Avenue.

Looking into the mirror and drawing a line with my sight down my body, I smile, satisfied with my choice.

Emerging from the bathroom, I see Knox lying on bed waiting for me. I attempt to stand provocatively against the door frame, and despite my slight stumble, I recover quickly.

His lips purse together to whistle, then he hisses a breath. "You know, baby pink is a classic choice."

The pink laced bodysuit is more like a one-piece swim-suit with clasps at the right spot to drive Knox wild.

Walking to bed, I slowly crawl on my hands and knees up the mattress. "I thought so too."

In one sharp movement, he flips me to the mattress and pins me down. "You drive me crazy." He begins to drag his teeth along the straps of the lingerie.

"I was going for that. Now, how about you get naked," I suggest as my hands begin to help him with the task.

He answers me with a kiss.

———

THE NEXT MORNING, I wake when I feel something wet licking my hand hanging from the bed. I'm lying on my stomach, as I slept this way after our last position choice of the night, but my eyes quickly make out Pretzel next to our bed.

"Knox?" My morning voice is thick with grogginess.

Knox rolls to his side and places his hand on my back. "Morning, shortcake." He too is waking up, as I hear him yawn.

"Why is Pretzel here? I thought you were picking him up later this morning when you have brunch at your brother's?"

Knox shoots up to sitting and looks to see Pretzel now staring at us as if he doesn't understand why we're still in bed. Even lets out a *woof*.

"Me too." Knox rubs his head as he wakes up. "Grayson must have dropped him off." He leans over to grab his phone on the side table. "Shit."

My stomach drops as I come to sit up and take the sheet with me.

"So, it seems the whole family is about to descend on us, as Blisswood brunch has had a change of location." He gives me an awkward smile.

"As in brunch with your brother. A brother. One brother?"

He laughs awkwardly. "Uhm, as in brothers, plural, and sister, plus kids, wives... you know, a small group." He quickly swallows and begins to look around for clothes.

I'm taking in this news. "Knox! I'm literally going to walk out into the kitchen, and they are all there?"

Knox leans over to kiss me. "Surprise." His voice is shaky.

Fuck me, I've just been thrown into an impromptu Blisswood family brunch.

19

KNOX

Not going to lie. I still enjoy making Madison squirm when I can, and her petrified face when I told her my family is waiting for us was fucking exhilarating.

Letting her have a few minutes to get ready, I quickly dressed and found myself walking into the kitchen of Olive Owl, desperate for a coffee to prepare myself for the ambush about to happen.

"Wow, you look like a man who is smitten." Grayson smiles as he sits and brings the mug of coffee to his lips.

I raise my brows at him. "Let me guess, it was your decision to move brunch here and an hour earlier than planned."

Bennett comes up from behind me and slaps a hand on my back. "Oh no, this was all my idea. Nothing better than catching my younger brother in a compromising scene. This is going to be fun."

This is payback, for sure, because games between us have always been our thing.

My eyes travel to my sisters-in-law Brooke and Kelsey.

Brooke is busy cooking at the stove but flashes me an entertained look, and Kelsey is holding her baby in one arm and mixing a Bloody Mary in the other.

Kelsey must pick up when I realize that alcohol is involved for today's menu. "Yep, we may need this." She too has a funny smile before she takes a bite of the celery stick that she had in her drink.

I shake off all their attempts to throw me off and walk to the coffeemaker. "Such a wonderful family, respecting boundaries and all," I say sarcastically.

"Hey! We legit need to do some stuff here this afternoon, and Lucy is checking on Cosmo with Rosie. We haven't prepared Lucy for the fact that her favorite English teacher is under your spell."

I set my mug down as I focus on pouring the coffee. "It's not a big deal. I will just be honest with Lucy and tactful. It's not like I'm going to say, 'Hey, Lucy, I'm sleeping with your favorite teacher.'"

The room goes silent, and I feel it in my bones that someone has entered the room. Turning slowly, I very quickly realize that Lucy is standing there with arms crossed and Rosie looking up at her aunt.

"Really, Knox? Really?" I can't read her face, and her tone is neutral.

Shit. This isn't how I was going to do this. But I've so got this.

I stand tall. "Yep. I'm…" What am I doing? Then it croaks out. "Dating Madison, Ms. Roads, Madison." Huh, what does Lucy call her?

"For how long?" She continues not to blink.

"I mean, do we really need to get into specifics?" My voice goes weak and cracks.

Lucy steps into the kitchen, and the thing about my

little sister is that she isn't afraid to dish out any disdain she may feel. Grayson and Bennett seem to lean back in their chairs, sipping coffee and enjoying the scene.

"Oh my God, Kendall was right, you and my teacher totally did it in the woods that one time and then you lied to me!" Her voice raises.

My hands quickly come up to defend myself. "No, I swear we didn't. We weren't sleeping with one another then."

I hear a communal groan.

"Are you kidding me, Knox? I don't want to know the fucking timeline of when you decided screwing my teacher was a perfect plan."

Brooke interjects with a spatula in the air. "Okay, kids, uhm… let's keep adult activity discussion to another time, as we have little ears here, and don't forget about language."

"Yeah, you owe me money for the swear jar!" Rosie pipes up and pulls on Lucy's sweater.

Lucy sweetly smiles as she looks at our niece. "That's okay, cutie, Uncle Knox is going to be paying my debts from now on. Don't forget to ask for inflation too." When Lucy looks up, her glare returns.

"It's not a big deal, Lucy." I'm over this now.

She shrugs a shoulder. "I guess it's not, it's just so… *weird*. I mean, you don't even date, you scr—" Lucy pauses and looks down at Rosie then returns her gaze to me. "You know what I mean."

"I do date," I proudly state. "I'm dating Madison. She's my girlfriend."

Fuck, did I just say that? Where did it come from?

Bennett coos out a sound then nudges Grayson's arm. "Now that's just cute."

"Little brother is maturing, does me proud." Grayson brings a hand to his heart.

"Can we all just be cool this morning?" I look around the room.

Crickets.

No promises or assuring looks.

I sigh and remind myself that this was coming at some point.

Everyone's eyes dart to the door.

"Morning," Madison greets everyone.

Quickly, I walk to her and wrap an arm around her from the side. "Relax. Weakness only makes them turn into wolves," I whisper into her ear.

"Good morning." Grayson tips his head up. Bennett waves.

"Hi there." Brooke gives a little curt wave, and Kelsey wiggles some fingers in the air.

There is a moment of raw awkwardness, and I realize we are all studying Lucy.

She steps forward and waves. "Right. You know me, your student. This is fine. I mean, whatever, weird, but fine. Can we just do this brunch now?" Lucy brushes everything off then walks toward the dining room.

"Shit. Is this really bad?" Madison whispers to me.

"Nooo." I drag it out as we all head to the dining room.

———

WE ALL SIT around the table and fill our plates with food.

Kelsey pours Madison a Bloody Mary. "It's either dinner or brunch every week, kind of tradition. Drew normally joins us, but I think he had a date last night." I hate that Lucy seems to struggle with hearing that fact, but Drew knows better than to go near my teenage sister, despite the fact they used to go to high school together. "Each week, we choose a different target. Sorry that it's your week without warning."

Madison takes a sip of her drink. "Whoa," she chokes out. "That's, uhm…"

Bennett chuckles. "Strong. Yeah, can't take the party girl out of the mama bear, amIright?" he proudly compliments his wife.

Madison laughs as she sets her glass down. "It's good. I will maybe take it easy if I plan on surviving this meal."

"Did you hear the news?" Grayson asks the table, and we all shake our heads.

"Someone here got a few big envelopes in the mail yesterday," Brooke proudly gushes as she reaches over to touch Lucy's arm.

I set my fork down. "College?" I ask Lucy.

"Yep. Two so far, early admissions and all." She can't hide her smile that she wants to flaunt.

"That's awesome." Madison looks so happy for her. "I knew you would get accepted."

"You should have told me sooner," I say as I grab a piece of bacon.

"Well, we were kind of occupied with your news of banging my teacher for my news to take precedence." Someone sputters their drink out. Lucy's eyes roam around the table. "It's fine, really. I'm cool with this," she assures all of us with a smile yet again.

"You sure?" Kelsey asks in humorous doubt.

"Totally," Lucy promises.

Ignoring my sister trying to rile me, I change the topic. "We should celebrate."

"Already on it." Grayson brings out a bottle of champagne from under the table.

Bennett gives a drum roll on the table, and everyone looks elated.

I lean over to Madison. "I swear we only let her drink when we're eating, and she isn't driving. We have a winery, so it's kind of odd not to let her, you know…"

Madison affectionately touches my arm. "Totally get it."

After a round of toasts, we continue to eat and discuss what life will be like with Lucy away from Bluetop. My sister is no longer a kid, and she's turning into a full-fledged adult, which is kind of bittersweet.

My attention turns to Madison next to me who is getting her ear chewed off by Rosie.

"Next year I go to the big-kid class and go a full day to school. I have to bring my lunch, but Mommy says I can pick my lunch box. Maybe by then I will have a brother or sister. Daddy says that if I ask Mommy nicely then she will agree, because I think I will be a good sister. I was made from magic, but Daddy says my brother or sister will be made from str- str…" Her words get stuck.

"Let me guess, strategic planning?" Brooke flashes Grayson a knowing look, and he just gives her his charming grin.

"Wow, sounds like you are excited. Do you read a lot of books?" Madison gives her full attention to Rosie.

"Lots."

"Good, I think I may have just the book for you. I will find it and give it to your mom."

"Cool."

"So, Madison, was it Knox's lack of manners that wore

you down?" Bennett asks as he throws a napkin on his plate.

I give him a warning glare.

Madison laughs it off. "Something like that. He did do some awful things to me to get my attention. Sent me for coffee at Sally-Anne's, tried to steal my pretzels, made me run a mile, and I am not entirely sure, but I think he bribed Helen to ensure I got stuck with him for the booster club."

"I'll never tell," I promise as my arm rests on the back of her chair.

She gives me a soft smile and brings her hand to my thigh. "It was also his determination and subtle abilities to show me he was interested that kind of wore me down. And I can't be certain, but I feel like he kept Pretzel because he knew that I would cry if he got rid of him. Then there is his soft side that he downplays."

"We're talking about this brother, right?" Lucy points her thumb to me.

"Yep."

"This is out of this world that we have a woman, an actual girlfriend, sitting at our family brunch gushing over Knox Blisswood," Bennett declares. "*And* the world is still turning." For once I can see he isn't joking, he's happy for me.

"I think it's great. Do you come from a big family?" Brooke innocently asks before she puts a forkful of eggs in her mouth.

"Not really. Must say, family meals like this are kind of new to me, but it's as fun as I imagined." Madison brings her shoulder to her ears.

"I hear ya. Kelsey and I also didn't really come from the big-family-meal-type families, but these guys kind of roped us into it. Created our own family, you know," Brooke explains.

Madison takes in her words then looks at me fondly. She's here for it, and I see her in every future dinner or impromptu brunch on the agenda.

"Can I spread the gossip at my salon that the last Blisswood brother is taken and claimed?" Kelsey asks as she looks into her nearly empty glass.

"Sure—"

Madison stops me with her hand. "Maybe wait until I tell my employer. But trust me, you can let loose when the time comes. Sophie Plums may need an update sooner than later," Madison jokes.

Kelsey looks like she struck gold with that comment. "Oh God. Did she proposition Knox too?"

"Wait, what?" Now I look at my brother in humorous shock.

"Yeah, at the gym," Bennett mentions.

We all laugh, and Lucy looks on like we are all crazy, but a grin dances on her lips.

"I like this one," Kelsey declares to me.

"Me too." I lean in to kiss Madison's cheek.

A half-hour later, I'm done clearing the table and walk into the kitchen where Lucy is sitting alone at the kitchen table and scrolling on her phone.

"We good?" I ask and slide onto the chair next to her.

She sighs and blows out a breath. "Yes, Knox, now stop asking."

"It's almost winter break, so maybe wait until after before sharing the news with your friends. Let Madison talk to Principal Beal. I'm not sure how it works, the whole teacher dating the hot brother of the student scenario."

Lucy rolls her eyes. "Requires better phrasing than that, for sure."

I touch her arm to ensure she looks at me. "I wasn't lying to you. It's new."

She studies me for a second, then her face relaxes. "I get it, and I'm not mad. It's kind of cool. I mean, I like her, and you are half-decent, so it seems like a good match. Just the second half of senior year kind of sucks already because I know what's going to happen when I graduate since I have my acceptance letters, and I have no big exams. And now the one interesting class that I have, my teacher is literally whispering sweet nothings into my brother's ear."

I grin at her logic. "Okay. One day, when you bring home the love of your life, then I promise I will go easy."

"I'll hold you to that... and you just mentioned love of your life." She stands and flicks my shoulder before leaving me to ponder my words.

———

Walking outside, I see that Madison is playing with Pretzel who is rubbing his back in the snow.

"Hey there." I wrap my arms around her from behind and kiss her cheek since she is covered in a coat, scarf, and a hat.

"Hey, *boyfriend*." She turns in my hold and drapes her arms against my shoulders. "You called me girlfriend earlier."

"Yeah." My face squinches. "Kind of went off script."

"Oh, so you're taking it back?"

"Hell, if you didn't get the memo that I would only put a woman through that interrogation if she meant something to me, then I wasn't clear enough, *girlfriend*."

"I'm not complaining. And they are good family, Knox, the best kind possible." She taps my nose with her mitten.

"You fit right in."

"I didn't feel a need to run away. I'm happy, Knox." Her words are a chain to my heart.

I lean down to kiss her and it's warm despite the cold winter day.

"This is new to me, but I want it," I promise.

"I hope so, because I need to navigate a few things to ensure that I'm not sent packing at the end of the school year," she explains, and I hear the disheartenment in her voice.

To me it's nothing, it will be fine. We have smooth sailing ahead, and even the subtle doubt in her smile doesn't faze me.

20

MADISON

O ver the winter break, I was in my own world… with Knox.

Over the last few weeks, we had long nights and lazy mornings.

Everything between us is moving along, and I spend my time at Olive Owl more than my own place, because I've come to realize that I don't like nights without Knox in it.

It's not that I've never had a relationship, I have. It's more that with Knox, it feels like there is always some edge to us; every day is exciting, even unpredictable. And I don't feel like it's just because we are new and in that phase of a relationship.

And here we are in January, back in the routine of the school year. I've been avoiding the inevitable and tried to press on with teaching, but the seniors are handing in some big reports next week, and I know my moral conscience won't let me grade Lucy's paper, even though I'm sure I could remain impartial.

Staring at Kendall standing in front of the class and

delivering a report on *The English Patient* is quite depressing. I know I said they could all pick a movie based on a famous book from the list that I gave, but the way Kendall mentions "the Harry Potter guy" Ralph Fiennes in a desert tells me she didn't really read or watch either.

My fingers glide along the skin of my neck as I listen, trying to soothe myself, then relief hits me when I look at the clock. "Thank you, Kendall, but I think we are short on time," I say from where I sit at the back of the class on a table.

"But I didn't talk about the mummy yet."

My heart breaks. "You mean when the man is hurt in a plane crash and they bandage his face?"

"Oh, is that what that was?" She looks confused.

Heaven help this generation.

Luckily the bell rings and I have students quick to escape. I should enjoy my three minutes of solitude, except when I walk to the door of my class, I stop in my tracks because I hear Lucy and Kendall outside in the hall chatting.

"Maybe I should just show up at his door on Friday," Lucy explains.

Kendall ponders, letting out a sound. "I don't know, I feel like Drew is really set on the whole being part of the Blisswood family thing he has going on. I think if he had to choose between you or your brothers then, well... sorry, Luce."

Oh fuckity duck. I don't need to hear this.

I step forward then back then forward, and I'm in a moral dilemma because I want to be the cool girlfriend of her older brother, but I should probably be the respectable role model who tells an almost-eighteen-year-old not to show up at the door of a twenty-one-year-old who I am positive had another date with some girl from the gym.

I go for it. I nearly tumble into the hall and save my fall. Casually wiping a hand through my hair, I say, "Oh, hey there, Lucy."

Kendall looks at me oddly before walking off, leaving Lucy to stare at me with the same bewilderment.

"You okay?"

"Totally. You know, I was thinking maybe Friday we could...Taco Friday, yep, let's do tacos with Knox."

Lucy crosses her arms over her chest. "You heard me, didn't you?"

I don't deny it. "Yeah, I did." I indicate with my head for her to move into my classroom.

She sulks back into the room, and I close the door behind me to see that Lucy is equal parts embarrassed and determined. "Look, Lucy, I'm not going to tell you it's a bad idea, because I think you know deep down it is. And I get that you and Drew are friends, because in normal circumstances the age difference isn't a lot, and you did go to school together at one point. But right now, seventeen and twenty-one is another realm. Different phases of life."

"And?" She gives me wide eyes as I perch on the edge of my desk.

"You're off to college soon, so many fish in the sea. Available fish too, who won't get bitten by the three sharks. You get me?"

"Yeah, you're treating me like *Finding Nemo*, fantastic." Her sarcasm makes me smile gently because it is completely a Blisswood gene. "You're going to tell Knox?"

"If you don't give me reason to then no, he doesn't need to know."

She studies me for a second. "Fine."

"Fine, you will take my advice? Or fine, you're trying to end this conversation?" I counter.

"The first one. I hear you. I'll just wait until I graduate and I'm eighteen." Lucy gives me a sly smile before walking off as students begin to enter my class.

My head falls into my hand as I sigh. Just let it be, I tell myself. She needs to discover life for herself, and I know Drew wouldn't do anything inappropriate.

Glancing behind me, I see the rows of students now sitting and remind myself that we have one more period, then I will speak with Principal Beal.

————

I FIDGET with the end of my sweater as I sit across from the principal who's sitting behind a desk. My eyes focus on the jar of wrapped toffees, and I notice how messy her desk is.

"What brings you by, Madison?" She offers me a warm smile.

"I thought we could discuss a minor matter that has developed," I begin confidently.

Her brows raise. "Oh?"

"Yes, you see, I really enjoy having Lucy Blisswood in my class."

"And, dear?"

I nervously smile. "However, I need someone else to grade her work."

Beal drops her pen onto the desk. "Great, so this happened." She doesn't sound thrilled.

"What do you mean?" I look at her curiously.

She leans forward with both arms on the desk. "I knew

Knox would charm his way into your world. Am I right?" Her look is stern.

"I'm allowed to see who I want in my personal life," I calmly reply but grip my skirt from tension building inside me.

"You are, but with the pare— you know what I mean, of your students is not ideal," she nearly scolds me.

"Knox isn't Lucy's legal guardian, and everyone seemed thrilled when we were thrown together for the sake of the booster club." I hear bitterness in my tone.

Beal begins to move some papers around. "Listen, I hear what you are saying, and who am I to stop young love, but not every parent will see it that way. I'm sure I will have parents calling to say that you have given Lucy special treatment."

"I haven't, I promise."

She holds her hand up. "I'm sure that's the case. But you did write her college recommendations."

"So did other teachers, and besides, when I wrote them then this wasn't an issue."

"Try explaining that to an overzealous parent of an honor-roll student."

I roll my eyes, as I understand what she is saying. "What am I supposed to do? Hide away during after-school hours?"

"Madison, I can't dictate your personal life, only advise you that parents are like eagles looking for prey. They use gossip to form reasons, and with those reasons, they strong-garm us, saying that their child should get this or that. Then they have the audacity to send us gifts at holidays to 'show appreciation' when really, it's a hidden agenda." She uses air quotes, and I try to take in her words.

"Okay, I understand that logic, but it won't affect my teaching," I implore and cross my arms over my chest.

Beal leans back in her chair. "I'm sure it won't, but parents complaining may affect your appraisal, and you need a good one in order to stay on next year."

My heart sinks because the mention of not having a job next year makes me nauseous.

"I'm going to a principal conference down in St. Louis for the next week. When I'm back we can discuss the consequences of this tidbit of information that you have shared."

Consequences? I'm in trouble? What the hell.

"Oh." I feel like I want to cry.

"Now if you'll excuse me, I need to look at the spring sports budget." She grabs her reading glasses and it's all the indication I need that this conversation is over.

———

KNOX HAS a wine tasting this evening, so he is finishing up with a group in the other room. I sit at the kitchen table of Olive Owl and stare down at Pretzel who has his head resting on my lap.

"I know, Pretzel, it isn't fair." I stroke the top of his head, and despite feeling a puddle of drool forming on my lap, I continue to shower him with affection.

The clearing of a throat has me look up to Knox who's standing in the doorway leaning against the frame. Wine-tasting Knox, with dark jeans and buttoned shirt, is my favorite, so incredibly sexy, and he always seems a little more commanding in bed when he plays wine connoisseur and business owner.

"You okay?"

"I guess."

"You ate half a block of cheese and crackers." He motions to the plate on the table next to me.

I shrug a shoulder. "Stress eating."

"Why?" He walks into the room and shoos Pretzel away so he can kneel down in front of me.

"I spoke with my boss today." My tone is full of fake enthusiasm.

He traps my hand between his own. "And? It's not a big deal, is it?"

"It isn't a small deal."

"Come on, that's ridiculous."

My eyes bug out at him that he brushes this off so easily. "It's really not. It could affect my appraisal, and Beal is worried what other parents may think. And if parents complain, then yeah, I'm in trouble, Knox, deep trouble."

He brings his thumb to my cheek to caress my skin. "That's crazy. You have done nothing wrong."

"If they don't renew my contract then I have no job, and no job means no Bluetop. Don't you see?" I try to make him connect the dots.

"It's not going to happen." He remains calm and even softly smiles at me as he rubs circles on the back of my neck.

"Easy for you to say. You are your own boss, and this will always be your home. Me? I'll have to find a new job during a time when there are a hell of a lot of college graduates who are eager to take a job at any price. There are also only so many opportunities in this county or the next county over."

There is a subtle tick of his jaw, and I wonder if it's because he realizes that I'm saying, that I want to stay near him, because that is a big chunk of the issue. I don't want to be away from him.

Knox moves to take hold of both of my hands, then he yanks me up out of my seat.

"Come on, shortcake, let's not think right now. Instead, let me distract you." He softly kisses the base of my throat then teases me by dragging his lips up my skin. "I'll do all the work. You won't need to lift a finger," he promises.

My entire insides are melting, and truthfully, his tactic may be helping in this very moment. A night of just me and him, no outside world, no clothes. It's the best avoidance there is.

He hauls me up and over his shoulder, fireman style, causing me to squeal in delight.

———

KNOX'S METHOD of distraction helped for a few days, but by the weekend, a worried feeling returned to my stomach. Not even the news when Grayson casually mentioned that Lucy stayed in Friday night was enough to make me smile.

Sitting across from Knox at Bear Brew with a croissant and cappuccino, I stare at him longingly.

"You okay?" He sips his coffee.

"Not really, no."

He reaches across the table to take my hand. "Relax."

"I can't. Maybe…" I bite my lip. I'm not entirely sure that I should mention the idea, but it could work.

"Maybe what?" he encourages me to continue, and his eyes look at me oddly.

An audible breath escapes me, and I decide to just

speak my mind. "Maybe we should cool down a bit, wait a little, you know?"

Immediately, he lets my hand go and a disgruntled scoff escapes his lips. The morning winter sun that shines through the windows only highlights the glare on his chiseled jawline.

"No. I don't know. In fact, wait, I do know. It's a fucking horrible idea." He's pissed.

I lick my lips, trying to compose myself, and scan the room to see that we are alone except for an old couple in the corner. "There is a lot on the line, Knox." I say his name with a bit of bite because I feel like he isn't even attempting to understand my frame of mind. "A job is what I need to pay off student loans, put a roof over my head, have something to do every day that I enjoy. Losing a job is a big deal."

"A job isn't a lot on the line, Madison. I can't even believe we are having this conversation." He shakes his head before angrily sliding his coffee cup to the side.

"Knox, that isn't fair. I'm not some woman who is going to wait for a husband then stay at home with the kids and cook you a three-course dinner every day."

His eyes widen from the attitude in my voice. "I know you aren't; you would only make a two-course dinner every day."

I grumble at his answer because he says it so seriously. "If we can't have a normal conversation about this, then really, I'm coffee-d out and would rather run two miles."

"Sure, don't get lost on the way to the parking lot like last time."

My mouth gapes open, as he is being a real asshole right now, but still... I stand my ground.

I rise from my chair and hope he says something meaningful. I even stall before moving another foot.

Instead, he sits there with a smug smirk, and it just riles me in both good and bad ways.

So I turn around and leave. "Call me when you get a damn clue, Knox."

21

KNOX

Sighing, I throw a wrench to the side. This morning, I woke to find that we had a leak near the barrel filter, and it should be an easy fix, except I'm in a foul mood.

The sound of the wrench landing on the ground causes Bennett and Grayson to stop working on their efforts and look at me.

"Great, we get Knox in a shitty mood," Bennett unenthusiastically declares.

"What's new? He's been this way all week," Grayson adds before returning to lay towels on the floor.

Rolling my eyes, I investigate if the leak has stopped. But really, I'm aggravated because it *has* been all week that I've been in this mood. Ever since Madison said we should cool down, to be exact.

We've been sending basic frosty-toned texts, and I'm confident we are avoiding one another, as we both seem to be busy suddenly.

"It's solved," I state, and I'm relieved at least one part of the day is turning out okay.

"The barrel or your mood? Because only one of those answers is convincing." Bennett raises a brow at me.

We all sit on the floor to take a break and I know a brother heart-to-heart is coming. How could it not?

"This is different, huh?" Grayson grins, and it causes me to widen my eyes in confusion. He continues, "Finally you get the 'don't do something ridiculous to jeopardize your relationship' talk."

"We are even having a relationship talk with Knox, so that's already earth-shattering," Bennett mentions as he rubs the stubble on his chin.

Looking between them, it annoys me that they're taking pleasure in this. Then again, I was the same when they each had their romantic lives implode.

"Let's get this over with," I puff out.

"Let's start with what's wrong? Is it still the whole thing, that Lucy is her student so some parents may be none too pleased and feel their little heathens are not getting enough attention?" Grayson asks as he opens his bottle of water to drink.

"Madison thinks we should cool down until the end of the school year." It's one-toned from my end because it deserves nothing more, because it's a horrible idea.

"Eek. Not only do you finally take a chance on a relationship, but she throws the cool-down card. She's really not following any of your usual protocols." Bennett scoffs a sound.

"I don't have usual protocols," I defend.

Grayson lets a sound of doubt escape. "Uhm, I think you do. First, they normally don't get past fuck-buddy territory. Secondly, they await at your beck and call, and finally, you are used to calling the shots. Except…" He waves a finger at me. "Madison is none of that. You waited for her, you wanted to upgrade the relationship, but she is the one suggesting something you don't like."

"What is it that you would like to highlight, Grayson? The fact that I'm completely mesmerized by a woman or the fact she has the ability to squeeze my heart in two?" I give him a pointed look.

"Fuck, he's using cutsie words. He said heart," Bennett teases me, because of course he would.

Grayson shakes his head at Bennett, unamused, then turns his attention back to me. "What does cool down even mean?"

"It means..." I think... wait... "See less of one another?" I question myself.

"Have you not further discussed this?" Bennett asks.

"Of course he hasn't, he's been stubborn and is waiting for Madison to grovel," Grayson informs us.

Bennett just starts to laugh. "Oh man, he's still like the kid who had a toy stolen and stayed upset until it was returned."

"Can you just be quiet?" I direct my attention to Bennett who lies back on his elbows.

"Not a chance. Because Madison is as stubborn as you and she won't beg. She's probably down in her mood like you, but she's staying put. You're both strong-willed and in a stalemate, but you will win," Bennett assures me. Looking at him with curiosity, I wonder how he reached that conclusion. He gives me a knowing glance. "Because you will show up at her door, confident and unfazed. Tell her that you are supportive of her and do whatever it takes."

"She wants to cool down, she obviously isn't invested," I admit my fear for the first time.

Grayson and Bennett look at one another then back at

me. "Maybe… or *maybe* she asked because she trusts that you two are the real thing."

"Besides, her not wanting to lose her job so she can stay in Bluetop is a fucking obvious clue." Bennett throws me a dirty towel that I catch.

That idea has been floating in my head, and truthfully, it feels good to hear someone confirming my thought.

"It's not that I don't understand her point. I just think it's a bit rash saying we should cool off. There are worst things that can happen in life."

We all look at one another in recognition, because death looms over us more than we like to admit. We watched our parents be taken too soon, and hell, I've watched my brothers create new families that was more cause for conflict than Madison saying to cool off. My situation is minor in comparison. I'm just…

Impossible.

"I just don't get it," Grayson says. "You do all the things you never did with a woman before, waiting and taking a chance. Yet this one tiny thing, a simple conversation with her, and you freak out. Come on, Knox, don't be this way," he chides me with a disapproving look.

"Yeah, lock in the stubbornness for another day," Bennett suggests.

I hold my hands up to get them to stop. "Okay, okay. I hear you."

For Madison, I will take the step forward. Go in confident and calm.

"Good. Now let's get out of here and grab some lunch, I'm starving." Grayson begins to shuffle up to his feet and we all follow suit.

We walk out of the warm inside to the outside cold, and

Bennett touches my shoulder. "Are you going to Madison's later?"

I laugh. "I'm all in on leading the conversation, but Madison is going to come to me. I have a plan."

Grayson stops in his tracks and looks over his shoulder to give me a pointed look. "What do you mean?"

I continue to walk forward, and I feel a smirk form on my mouth. "Nothing crazy. I mean, it may need to involve rope, but that's a given. Can't have her getting out of hand, can I?"

Grayson looks horrified, meanwhile Bennett just chuckles. "Oh man, why am I not surprised?"

"I've got this, don't worry," I promise as we head inside to grab lunch.

———

MADISON STANDS tall with arms crossed and giving me a once-over as she tries to figure out what is happening. "Okay, you said Pretzel wasn't feeling well and that I should come here."

It was easy.

I faked a Pretzel-is-sick story and Madison came running. But now we are both staring at the dog gnawing on a giant piece of steak, because he's a good boy and he's my dog, so he deserves the best.

I swipe my hand through my hair as I look at Madison whose disproving look may burn a hole through the floor of the kitchen at Olive Owl. She's steaming in the fact that I got her here under false pretenses. "I know you want to kill me that I used him as a ploy, but now that you are here..."

Her eyes bug out, but I'm going to go for this.

I grab her and sling her over my shoulders with her feet kicking in protest. "Put me down now, Knox!"

"Nope," I say as I take us in the direction of my room.

I can hear her smile through her grumbles as she kicks and wiggles in my hold.

Arriving in my room, I set her down, and her eyes immediately blink when she sees the chair sitting in the middle of the room.

I break her attention by unbuckling my belt with one big woosh sound when I pull it out. I can see her shiver.

"What is this?" I'm still unsure if she is all game or really unimpressed. "B-belt? Really?"

"You're still annoyed with me from the other day, and I need you to cooperate." I step to her and gently press against her shoulders with my fingertips until the back of her knees hit the chair. She sits down and looks at me curiously. "Allow me?" I double-check, trying to suppress my grin. But truth be told, I know this is one of her fantasies because it slipped out once on our drive to the city.

"I'm positive this is partly kidnapping, but since I'm here, I might as well play along." A closed-lip smile is faint on her mouth before she willingly brings her wrists behind the chair.

Our eyes remain locked as I start to work on the belt to tie her wrists to the furniture—a little tight.

"This is all for the greater good." I caress her cheek with the back of my finger. "Trust me, you need to learn a lesson, teacher."

"Oh, do I?" She's sassy today as she dangles her arms that can't be set free and looks around the room.

I shouldn't be entirely turned on by the fact that she looks extremely hot or that I can't wait to taunt her and touch her, but I have to remember that first we need to talk.

Leaning down, I brush her hair behind her shoulders. It's extra thick, shiny, and bouncy today, since she just came from Kelsey's salon. It will feel great against my chest after Madison and I debate for a while, then she comes a few times and nuzzles into me the way she does.

She wants to smile, but instead she swallows and tries to sit tall. "I knew you were bad news when I met you."

I lick my lips, amused. "And yet you still like me. Let's begin…"

22

MADISON

I observe the man circling me, completely in control of this situation, his smirk never fading. Admittedly, this gets points for creativity, but I need to ask the obvious. "A talk over coffee wouldn't have sufficed?"

Knox chuckles softly and leans down so we are at eye level. "Nah, this is more our style."

"Is it?" I raise a brow. "I'm positive that I much prefer you apologizing on your knees. Say it with me. S-O-R-R-Y."

"But I am on my knees." He drops to the floor in front of me and his hands land on both sides of the chair. I am truly trapped and bounded down under him. "I'm just not going to say sorry," he taunts.

I grumble a noise out of frustration because now I realize that I have to listen to him, and it won't be what I was expecting for him to say.

"Enlighten me then, what the hell is this?"

"You can apologize to me," he casually mentions as his fingers crawl up my arms until his finger bops the tip of my nose.

Shaking my head, I'm now very annoyed. "I have nothing to apologize for."

He stands up and he is now slightly aggravated. "Madison, we are too good together to be in a dispute because of miscommunication."

Not entirely wrong.

"Where was that philosophy the other day? Huh? Because, Knox, I don't want to end up having to leave Bluetop. Sure, I like my job, but there is this incredibly frustrating obnoxious man who ties up his girlfriend to discuss serious topics, and I think I may miss him if I was forced to leave." I roll my eyes to the side.

With his hand on his hip, his other hand rubs his chin with a bit of stubble, God, I love his stubble. "A job is a job, Madison. You could get sick or worse tomorrow and that is something more important than a job."

A sharp breath cuts me off as I realize where his train of thought comes from. How could I have not connected the dots? Because underneath Knox Blisswood's steely exterior, he has had to deal with a lot in his life. He just never shows anyone that he has been affected.

"All I'm asking is we wait before we grow even closer, or I don't know… If we are meant to be, then what's a few more months? Can't you wait? Or will you lose interest? I mean, I will be there waiting in the end—" He cuts me off by slamming a kiss on my mouth.

Holy moly, it's hard to be unable to move my hands to touch him as he devours my mouth. Knox's kiss when he tries to prove a point does something to my soul; my whole body just melts into his demand.

Pulling away, he's kneeling with his hand on my face and his eyes sincere. "No way would I lose interest, but I'm not a patient man. I do think you shouldn't let it bother you so much.

Beal has no grounds to fire you, and the parents will always find something to bitch about. But..." His thumb runs along my bottom lip in a soothing fashion. "What if I have a better idea?"

"I have no choice but to listen, you tied me up." I hear the humor in my tone as the corner of my lip stretches a line.

"Might need to spank you too." Knox flashes me a devilish grin before he runs his lips down my neck, and his head nuzzles lower and lower until his fingers unbutton my jeans. "The thing is, shortcake." He unzips my jeans. "I'm not going to say sorry, you're not going to say sorry." His fingers hook under my waistband, with my entire body turning sensitive and needy. Then Knox kisses below my navel and my body bucks under him. "So, let's agree that we both want the same thing." His lips move lower.

I breathe out a breath, trying to calm myself down. "I may be up to this negotiation."

My jeans are peeled off and then Knox is stationed between my legs, urging my knees to part open, and he kisses the bend of my leg. "Because you make me do things I would never do for anyone, then I will compromise."

"Wow, big steps for Knox."

His tongue darts out and draws a fucking heart on my skin. *Cute.*

"We can cool down... in public. But behind closed doors then it's business as usual." Knox resumes kissing up and ever so closely to the intimate area that is craving him desperately right now.

"That's the problem, Knox," I admit and bite my lip. His eyes peer up at me, and he pauses in his quest. "I like you too much. I'm too obvious, even when we are apart. People who sneak around always get caught."

"You managed it well before we were official."

I laugh as my feet and legs wrap around him to keep him close. "Maybe that's the thing, we weren't official. We were a curiosity, we detested one another, it wasn't certain where we would end up. At that point, murder could have been an option. All cards were on the table."

"Ah, so being official has Madison all weak."

I look away. "Let's not make a big deal about this."

"We are compromising, so give me a counteroffer," he suggests.

I look at him with a puzzled expression. "How about holidays?"

"Holidays?"

"We can text and run into one another randomly in Bluetop. But secret rendezvous will only take place on holidays. It will keep us in check and fill the void until the end of May when the school year ends."

"It's January, what the hell?" He sighs and stares at me for a few seconds. "Which holidays? Valentine's day, St. Patrick's, Easter, that doesn't give us much."

I hum a sound. "Anyone in your family Jewish?"

"Nope. Why?"

"Hmm, would have given us a few extra holidays," I explain my logic, and it causes him to smile.

"Damn it... Okay, we can't forget about Groundhog Day."

"Naturally, I mean, that's a crucial holiday, maybe the most important of the year," I agree far too seriously.

"Spring break, that's for sure on the table, right?" He looks at me with hope.

I shake my head no. "That's not really a holiday, plus I have a few workshops for the Juniors before they take their

SATS in the spring. Besides, spring break is more a college thing."

He fakes a pout. "No Madison in a bikini on a beach in Cancun?"

Again, I shake my head. "Are we really going to do this?"

"Yes… if I get to negotiate a few points, and we have." His fingers run along the skin of my thighs in an affectionate way.

"Why are we doing this again?"

"Because we are not a mis-communicative couple, we are a negotiate-and-compromise couple."

I shake my wrists. "Then unbuckle me."

"Nope." He shimmies back onto his knees and his mouth returns to my skin. "Now, can we confirm that we ended up here because you don't want to leave me, and I think we are strong enough to handle anything?" Knox doesn't wait for my answer before sliding my lace panties to the side.

"Yes," I breathe out right before he stands, leaving me wide and open.

Circling behind me, he leans down, with his breath landing next to my ear. "I love when you are agreeable."

His fingers sneak under my shirt collar, and he moves the bra cup down, but his fingers quickly cover my nipples.

"I can't get enough of you," he murmurs against that soft spot below my ear.

Squirming underneath him, I can't do much else, as I am at his mercy. "Knox, please… the belt." I squeal out a sound as he pinches my nipples.

"Hmm, you did say please." His hand takes hold of my neck, and he guides my gaze up to him. He offers my mouth to his for a kiss filled with connection and command that he is my captor.

My entire body wants to break free from this chair so I can mount him and take control of this situation. Hell, I'm not even sure what position we could do in this set-up.

"Belt," I request again.

His tongue clicks against the top of his mouth. "Thinking about it."

Knox brings his other hand out from underneath my shirt and he slides it down my body, causing tingles along every fiber underneath my navel and between my legs, before his finger sweeps between my folds, causing me to gasp.

"You are always ready for me." His fingers swirl in my juices, and the moment he circles my bundle of nerves, a long moan escapes me, and my body coils want in my center.

"Need more?" He whispers his question.

I swallow and try to remain composed. "I wouldn't complain."

His finger dips inside of me as his thumb takes over my clit. My body arches off the chair and the sound of my labored breath fills the room.

Why does this man have such power over my body, so incredibly wicked and wonderful?

"Seriously, untie me *now*," I seethe out, as I can't sit still.

"Still contemplating."

"Contemplate faster," I urge.

Another finger disappears inside of me while his other hand clenches my jaw. "You want fast? Or should I pull your hair and fuck your beautiful mouth?"

"Fuck, Knox, I don't want to play this game anymore."

He is quick to circle back around and land on his knees in front of me. "What about this game?" His mouth lands on my pussy, and immediately my head falls back with my eyes closing as I see stars explode behind my lids.

What world am I in that my boyfriend has me tied to a chair and he is fucking me with his tongue?

And why does it turn me on so much, nor am I complaining if this were to happen again?

I pant out his name as he continues his quest on my clit. In true Knox fashion, he doesn't stop until he has me shaking from the earthquake that he causes, my entire body trembling from my orgasm as his tongue strokes me until I calm.

Sitting there, my chest visibly moves up and down as I try to return to earth.

Finally, I look down as Knox reluctantly pulls his face back and brings his thumb to wipe the corner of his mouth to taste every last drop that is on his lips.

"I *really* enjoy you like this." His eyes are sinfully satisfied.

"If this is how every disagreement is going to go then I need to find more things that annoy us," I drowsily say as I breathe out a calming breath.

He chuckles at my thought. "Still want me to untie you?"

I squint an eye at him. "Is that a trick question?"

"Nah, I figure you may want to move this to the bed or you over my knee for that spanking, plus I know you like to use your hands when I'm fucking your mouth."

His vulgar mouth is my undoing.

Knox walks on his knees and unbuckles the belt. "Shit," he curses.

My wrists fall free, and I shake them off as I bring them

forward. "Knox, these marks really better disappear before I talk to Beal." I rub the red lines around my wrists, the print that screams I did something kinky this weekend.

"It will be fine in a few hours," he promises.

My head perks up from his comment. "Oh my God, this isn't your first time doing this to someone?"

He laughs then gives me an assuring grin. "I have brothers, and we tortured one another growing up. Not to mention, the day Lucy says she found the one then he is getting full-on interrogation, including mind games."

I burst out laughing as he comes to tenderly kiss my wrists before he slides me off the chair into his arms, carrying me to his bed.

Lying down on our sides facing each other, we lock eyes as I slowly work his pants free because I am still half-naked and it doesn't feel like an equal playing field.

"Tell me again, we will be alright," I request.

He brushes hair behind my ears. "It'll be agonizing, but we have a middle ground." Knox lets a groan out as my hand takes hold of his hard cock.

"Thank you for making us talk, although slightly unconventional. But don't involve Pretzel ever again," I warn him.

"You wouldn't have shown up here otherwise, because you're stubborn," he reminds me, and I squeeze his length harder for his comment.

"Let's not debate it anymore. I believe I need to punish you for that stunt you just pulled."

His hand spanks my ass causing a delicious sting to the skin. My mouth opens from the surprise.

"Ooh, I thoroughly agree, do your worst." He grins as his fingertips glide up my obliques and take my shirt with.

But I'm not going to make him lie there in agony for

too long. Instead, my leg props over his hip, pulling him closer to me, his cock finding home between my legs.

"Nah, you expect that. How about we just move slowly, *very* slowly." Our heads fall onto one another's shoulders as he enters me, and my internal walls envelope around his length.

"I'm only going to agree." He nips the skin of my neck as we move together in slow thrusts.

Our lips fuse together as we get lost and relish the evening, knowing things are going to be a little different in the months ahead.

I've never taken my foot off the accelerator in a relationship unless it was to end one, but that isn't my intention with Knox. And I know anything less than speeding isn't Knox's way. But then again, he swears he's never even been in a relationship like ours.

And I'm curious if it really will be okay.

23

MADISON

I arrive confidently in Principal Beal's office and sit down, determined to make my point.

"Madison, I suppose this has to do with what we discussed the other week?" she says as she takes her glasses off.

"Yes. You can't fire me for being with Knox, but I understand your concerns about what some of the parents may think, especially as Lucy is really smart and will most likely be top of her class. And even though Lucy doesn't care—nor any of the Blisswoods, for that matter—I appreciate the sensitivity to this situation." I speak rehearsed and focused, straightening my pencil skirt.

Principal Beal looks at me with interest and seems to be listening. "I'm not against you and Knox, dear. I know those Blisswood men have their ways, and kudos to you for getting the wild one to settle down. I hope I get an invite to the wedding one day, really. It's the parents of Bluetop's future generation that I am concerned about."

"I know, and while I don't agree with hiding my

personal life. I will be sure to stay on the down-low so nobody can make an issue."

"Rumors are already flying," she informs me.

I shrug a shoulder. "There are always rumors in this town, but I won't give them any reason to confirm them."

Beal nods her head then puts her glasses back on. "Good, sounds like a plan then. Mr. Jones will grade Lucy's work going forward and will have to sit in on her presentations, and you can explain to your students that he needs to do that for your appraisal, partly true." She tips her head to the side.

"Okay." I stand up. "Assuming we aren't going to talk about getting snacks in the teachers' lounge, then I think this conversation is done."

She smirks as she begins to read a document. "We are indeed, Ms. Roads."

"Have a good day," I say before leaving.

Sighing, I make my way to my classroom, and I see that Lucy is leaning against the door waiting for me.

"Hey, Lucy, everything okay?" I ask as I take out my keys.

Lucy propels off the door. "Yes, but Knox filled me in on the new plan. You really have him in a way that I've never seen before. He is almost like a cuddly teddy bear."

If only she knew what he did to me this weekend.

I smile politely. "How so?"

"I don't know, he just seems completely... in love."

A flutter in my heart causes my pulse to quicken. "I care for him, Lucy."

"I hope so. He doesn't take chances on women, yet here he is, doing just that."

I only tip my head up in acknowledgment as I open the door.

"Anyway, I don't have to move classes, do I?"

"No, you don't, you're fine." We walk to my desk. "You haven't mentioned your brother and me to your friends, have you?"

Lucy indicates with her fingers by zipping her lips. "Only Kendall saw you two that one time at the forest preserve, but apparently that was nothing. And besides, then she would have to explain to her parents why she was there at that time of day when she was supposed to be at my place."

I laugh at her sentence as I unpack my drawer.

"And what about you, Lucy? I mean, there isn't a guy I need to keep Knox away from, is there?"

Lucy's face goes slightly stiff, as she knows I'm onto her determination to pursue the honorary Blisswood brother, Drew.

"Well, look at the time." She smiles and glances at a pretend watch on her wrist.

I grin as she walks back out of my class. "Bye, Lucy."

She waves without turning to look at me. Sitting down at my desk, I glance at my phone, and I quickly send a text to Knox to let him know that I spoke to Beal. It doesn't take long for him to return my message.

Knox: Cross that off the list, and start the countdown to days filled with blue balls and you pining over me. Okay, so I did a search, and apparently, we really need to celebrate Squirrel Appreciation Day. It's a thing, and I really feel like we underestimate their power to take over the world.

Me: We agreed on Valentine's Day, St. Patrick's, Easter, and Groundhog Day... that's it.

Knox: So I should take World Book Day off the list? I mean, that seems right up your alley.

I smile to myself. He researched this, he's invested. Even throws in a few writing emojis.

Me: Knox!

Knox: Fine.

There is an emoji with arms crossed.

Knox: See you on Groundhog Day. If he sees his shadow, then let's stay in bed longer.

Me: I can agree with that.

Knox: Okay. I guess I need to up my romantic holidays game.

Me: You literally run a winery that wins awards for being a romantic destination. I'm sure you can manage.

Knox: No pressure or anything.

Me: Have to run. You'll figure it out. Hug Pretzel for me.

Looking up, I see teenagers entering class looking tired and dreading the day ahead.

Truthfully, I feel their pain, because for once we share the same mood.

———

GROUNDHOG DAY WAS A TOTAL BUST, to be honest. I had the flu, so any plans for a romantic rendezvous were replaced by Knox bringing me soup and watching me sleep after I downed some Nyquil and was out like a light. In fact, there were no sexy times for us at all.

Which means for Valentine's Day that I need to make it up to him, because our time is precious and scarce. We need to make it extra special.

So here I am, looking at his bed where he has left me a giant heart-shaped box of chocolates, and I debate how I should lie to wait for him. Valentine's Day and wine go hand in hand, and there is a wine tasting happening all night that Knox and his brothers need to run, which is why it's 10pm and he sent me straight to his place with a wink and a promise that he wouldn't be much longer.

Throwing my coat and bag to the side, I'm grateful that this holiday falls on a weekend, which means we can technically extend it to the morning in terms of holidays. Stripping down to my underwear and bra, I look in the mirror, satisfied with my dark red lace choice.

But it's kind of cold, so I grab his sweatshirt without hesitation and throw it on with a plan that when I hear him approaching the door, I can pull it off and get into my attempt of a sexy position.

Flopping onto the bed, I stare curiously at the chocolate box and open it. So many options, and a few chocolate-covered pretzels too, and I pop one into my mouth. When my phone pings, I look at the screen.

Knox: Almost done. Half hour tops. Help yourself to the chocolates, but I know you already are!

Me: I am totally not... eating all of them. Sure! Take your time. This feels kind of like a booty call haha.

Knox: Don't worry, it will be more than your booty getting attention...

He knows me too well. I take a bite of one square and realize I don't like the white cream filling, so back into the box it goes, and then another with hazelnut. I should probably pace myself, stuffing my face with delicious chocolates. Knowing I can probably finish my chapter that I was reading earlier, I grab my book from the bag and begin to read the romance about the hockey player falling for the friend's younger sister—always a classic.

I'm not sure what happens, but my eyes blink open to the feeling of arms around me. My eyes draw a line from the hand resting on my belly, up the arm, to my favorite man smirking at me.

It dawns on me what is going on.

"Oh no! I fell asleep." I shoot up to sitting.

Knox's low chuckle tells me he is amused. "You did. I arrived to find you with a very dirty book open and a box of half-eaten chocolates, you in my sweatshirt, and yeah, I noticed the lace on underneath." He cocks his head to the side on the last part.

My hand covers my face. What a way to make an impression.

"So incredibly sexy, everything about it." He slowly moves to trap me under him by placing his knees on each side of me and resting his hands against the headboard. "You waiting in my bed." He slants his head then leans in to kiss my lips. "In my sweatshirt." Another kiss. "Did you touch yourself?" he whispers.

I laugh and tease. "Because of the book or waiting for you?"

His mouth nips my cheek as he murmurs a sound, right before he grabs my arms and pulls me on top of him as he falls back.

"I'm sorry I fell asleep. What time is it?" I ask as I rest my head against his heart.

Knox begins to stroke my hair with his hand, and he places a kiss on the top of my head. "It's okay, I was a bit later than I'd planned, and I think it's now 11:30. I enjoy watching you sleep, even better when it's like that."

"I was going to go for the whole sexy seduction scenario," I admit. "Instead, you get me, a blob in your bed. There is probably chocolate melted onto the sheets somewhere."

"You're my girlfriend, I'm allowed to see you like this.

And I know we always want to be on our A-game with one another, but this is also perfect. We can sleep if you want, and I'll ravish you in the morning after breakfast in bed." I love the way he says it all like it's so easy and simple. It's because he means it.

I look up at him as my chin rests on my hands splayed on his chest. "Knox, you just knocked my fictional hockey player out of my head, a hard thing to do. You really have a way of explaining things; I would never have imagined this soft and sensitive side to you when I first met you."

His eyes bulge out. "Whoa, whoa, whoa, Madison Roads. Let's keep the sensitive and soft perception to between these four walls, and when you met me, you had no idea who I was except for a possible incarnation of the devil."

Moving to straddle him, I have a mischievous grin on my lips. "Oh, but you are sometimes, and I love it. Now I believe we have to make the most of this holiday, so how about…" I slowly peel his sweatshirt up and off to reveal my lace number, and he groans and tilts his hips up to let me feel his emerging cock. But then I reach over to the box of chocolates. "We finish these chocolates then get some shut-eye."

"I'll do whatever you want, woman, as long as you let me stare at you." Knox grins.

We both shuffle to sitting, facing one another, and he grabs his phone to put music on the Bluetooth as I drag the box of chocolates between us.

"Take your shirt off, Knox." I give him a warning glare.

If I'm going to sit here in lingerie, then he needs to shed some fabric. He gives me an agreeable look before following my demand.

"Fair is fair," he states, throwing the shirt to the side

before squinting his eyes at the box of chocolate squares with bite marks in every piece because I was indecisive.

I like this. Just being together, eyes wandering and silence comfortable.

"Big crowd?" I ask about the wine tasting.

"Yeah, every year it's the same. Can't miss a business opportunity, though. I mean, Valentine's has always been big here."

"I know, I've heard. And now I have proof that you were not just playing a part for business, you have moves."

"I just never shared them with anyone." Our eyes catch. "Until now," he assures me before leaning in for a kiss.

I hum my satisfaction with that remark. "Tell me something that I don't know, Knox," I request.

He pauses as he throws a chocolate into the box. "I think… well, I *know* my brothers have been in their own world recently with the families they've created, and while I don't envy the raising-children part, they are so incredibly happy it's hard not to want to envy that. And I think now more about what life will be like in five years than I ever did."

I touch his arm. "That's a natural feeling to have. It's called personal growth," I tease. "And I know what you mean, except I think I've always thought about life in five or ten years. It's kind of like my life now in Bluetop. I'm a homebody and I like the quiet, but it will be better to share it with someone and possibly procreate a little mini-me," I reflect.

There is a long silence until he says something that catches me off guard.

"You make me want things, Madison." His tone is steady and firm.

I think I nearly blush. "Even though I'm making us see less of one another?"

He slides everything on the bed to the side, pulling me close with our hands connected. "Your tactic is fucking driving me crazy, because I only think of you and want you more."

"So you're not losing interest?" My heartbeat hurries.

"Absolutely not. I'm turning into a crazed man who is impatiently waiting to make you mine for the world to see."

I throw my arms around his neck. "I'm falling in love with you." Then I freeze.

My mouth can't close when I realize what I just declared, meanwhile a soft smile forms on his lips.

"I'm not going to argue with you on that. I don't even know what falling in love is, but I'm going to guess it's something like this, and I'm nearly there."

I appreciate his honesty. I'm not even sure what we just committed to one another. It was an almost I love you, so close but still fleeting.

Our lips press against one another for a long kiss, a deep kiss, a confirmation.

"How am I not inside of you yet?" he rasps into my ear before pinning me to the mattress, and I shriek in delight. "I retract what I said earlier. No sleeping. We are going to be fully awake. We have a lot to accomplish, because the next time we get this is St. Patrick's Day."

"Three and half more months, we've got this," I state as my breath grows labored.

The subtle tick of his upper lip confirms that he knows, but it also concerns me, because deep within me, I know there is the fear that he won't hold out for so long.

But I can't think right now.

24

KNOX

Throwing a queen of hearts onto the table, I look around at my brothers and Drew while we play poker in Grayson's house.

Kelsey and Brooke are in the kitchen, probably talking about the fact we all just watched Lucy get picked up for prom wearing a purple dress that got all our approval. All afternoon she was with Brooke and Kelsey getting ready, then her date got the third-degree from Grayson when he arrived, while Bennett and I watched on, amused. Luckily, Lucy is going with a friend, and I am 100% positive that nothing is going on between her and Sean from the baseball team.

"I'm out." Bennett throws his cards on the table.

"Are we actually playing or just pretending to play?" Drew asks, skeptical, before taking a sip of his beer. He arrived because Bennett and I have every intention of playing cards while babysitting.

"Well, I have nothing to lose." And I don't mean just the cards.

I'm a little lost in general, yet completely focused; can

you be both? Who knew slowing down could bring you closer with someone?

"Brooke and I need to head out in about ten minutes." Grayson breathes out. He is dressed in a crisp white shirt and dark blazer.

"Okay, the kids are asleep, Pretzel is with Rosie in her room, and the wine is open," Kelsey states as she arrives in the room with a bottle of our white, then slides right onto Bennett's lap.

Grayson looks at his wife with a playful grin. "Chaperone duty awaits."

"Really?" Bennett says. "When Helen asked if you could chaperone prom, you decided to be one of *those* adults who decides to embarrass their kid, in this case, our sister?" he yet again scolds Grayson.

Brooke smiles as she seems to be checking the ribbon on her dark blue dress. "I guess it will be fun. I mean, it's a little bit of a throwback to our high school days."

"Yeah? Sounds like the backseat of your car may need to be cleaned tomorrow," I mumble a quip.

My oldest brother gives me a death glare since he heard me well enough. "Don't be in a foul mood."

My head perks up. "I'm not."

In truth, I think I may be jealous. Grayson chaperoning prom means sharing the responsibility of the night with teachers, teachers like Madison who I know will be there because she got roped into duty by Beal who said it's her first year, so there is no debate.

"Okay, you're not in a foul mood, my bad. You're walking around like a lovesick puppy. We never thought we would see you in love so soon. I mean, we thought we had at least another few years of you being, well, a single bachelor. But now you are a man rooted down and absolutely loving that idea."

"True, Knox has gone soft on us," Bennett adds. "It's adorable, this whole seeing one another only on holidays thing. You are a man drunk on love."

Drew just shrugs his shoulders at me, as he doesn't want to get involved.

"Am I now? I don't feel like someone who is waking up elated every morning. I'm tied down to a schedule and have to wait two more months to break free of these chains." I grumble from the thought.

"But you're waiting and that is quite a monumental step; you must really feel something for her," Drew mentions as he slides his bottle of beer to the side.

"I do, but yeah…" I can't pinpoint what has me bothered in this moment. All the guys look at me to finish my sentence. "I feel like she is in control of the relationship."

Bennett sputters out his beer and Grayson just laughs, meanwhile Drew gives me an odd look.

Bennett shakes his head at me, truly entertained. "Are you kidding me? That is what has you gloomy? You don't get to be dominant for a hot second and it has you out of sorts. Nah, that's not it."

"No, I don't buy it, that's not the issue," Grayson explains. "This is all new to you, Knox. Not even just the relationship part, it's that it's a relationship that *matters*. She's the one."

Drew decides to chime in. "From what I can tell she totally is your other half. You two can do the whole Little House on the Prairie thing once Lucy graduates."

Brooke looks at him, surprised.

Drew shrugs. "I remember reading it once in elementary school."

Kelsey's face lights up. "Oh my goodness, yes! You two will live at Olive Owl and it's perfect."

Sitting with them all right now is giving me a headache. I don't enjoy sitting on the sidelines. That's all I've been doing lately, waiting and waiting. It isn't me.

"Let's head out," Grayson says as he places a hand on his wife's lower back. "Helen will crucify us if we're late. We'll say hi to Madison for you, Knox."

"Wait!" I shout. The entire room looks at me. "I'll do chaperone duty."

"Since when?" Grayson asks.

Drew shakes his head. "Since he decided he wants to follow a bad idea."

I stand up off my chair. "I want to see Madison. She said holidays, plus Bluetop is small, so we may randomly run into one another. I'm following her rule."

"This isn't random. It's calculated, with her *colleagues* around, on *prom* night for our *sister,*" Grayson blankly reminds me.

"And?" I ignore his attempt to change my mind. "I filled in on chaperone duty before and nobody cared."

"Uhm, positive that was before you decided that sleeping with our sister's teacher was a great idea," Bennett reminds me.

I give everyone a pointed look. "I'll be discreet, it's fine."

"Really?" Grayson is still doubting me. "Then why only come up with this plan now? What's gotten into you?"

I bite my bottom lip as I think about what emotions are swirling inside of me, but I'm not going to get into the details right now.

"I don't think anything you say will change his mind," Drew chimes in. "I see it in his eyes, he's a man on a mission." He throws his cards onto the table, giving up on the idea that any games will be played.

Grayson rubs the bridge of his nose because he knows Bluetop High just gained another chaperone.

———

MY SISTER LOOKS AT ME, slightly enraged, as she drags me to the corner of the ballroom of the hotel along the river in Bluetop. I quickly went home to change and showed up ready to chaperone, but I am a little late, as the night is already underway.

"Are you kidding me right now? It was bad enough having Grayson volunteer to chaperone, but I could justify it because he helps Coach Dingle with the baseball team, people want him here. You?" Lucy brings her hand to her forehead then leans closer to me to loudly whisper, "The entire cheerleading squad thinks you're hot. This is so fucking uncomfortable."

"Relax," I assure her. "I'm not here for you. I know you drink responsibly and won't disappear to a hotel room with the Seanster."

She cringes at my words. "I know you're not here for me. That's fucking obvious."

My eyes scan the decorated room with blue lighting and seniors dressed up for the special occasion.

"Just do whatever you came here to do then *leave,*" my sister urges before rolling her eyes and storming off.

I smile to myself, because underneath her annoyance, she is cool enough to let this all go by tomorrow.

Searching the room, I spot Madison standing along the side. The French teacher, Sebastian, here on a three-month exchange program, is talking to her; I've seen him at the gym benching far less than me.

I don't like his eyes on her, not one bit, but I know Madison wouldn't give any indication of interest. To most people Madison is single, but she's standing before him in a black dress that I want on my floor, though I'm sure most would consider it conservative enough.

People really underestimate the power of a knee-length dress, a crime really.

It takes me no time to arrive next to Madison, whose polite smile drops when she realizes I'm standing there. Her eyes tell me she is surprised and concerned that I'm here.

"Good evening, Ms. Roads." I flash her my best look.

"Mr. Blisswood." She gulps. Looking between Sebastian and me, she's unsure what to do. "What a *surprise* to see *you* here. I thought Grayson was gracing us with his help tonight." Her smile is tight, awkward, and I fucking love it.

I can only smirk confidently. "I'm filling in. I'm sure Helen won't mind, I've helped before."

Madison looks at Frenchie who's watching us, intrigued. "Excuse us, I need to… brush Mr. Blisswood up on… rules, which rules we need to make sure the students follow. Yep, that." Her hand grips my arm, and to the Frenchie it's a sweet pull, but I feel some claw action happening.

When we are away from other people, but still able to watch the room, she lets me go. "What the hell, Knox?" she whispers in a panic. "What are you doing here?"

"I need to talk to you. So be it if in order to do it, I have to stop eighteen-year-olds from sneaking in alcohol or going upstairs to lose their virginity. I'll hate it, but if it means I get to be with you, then I'll do it."

Madison smooths her hair that is hanging down, luscious, and ugh, I want to wrap it around my hand.

"Does Helen know you're here? Principal Beal? I mean, fuck, I can't be in a room like this with you looking like… that." She points to me.

"This?" I look down at myself and pull my suit jacket open slightly. I ditched a tie.

She licks her lips and looks around the room slightly frazzled. "The button-down and your hair today is just, well, it's kind of hot. Like, really hot, distracting. *So* distracting." Madison is adorable when she's flustered.

I step closer to her so only she will be able to hear. "You mean like St. Patrick's Day distracting, when you said you were wearing green but I had to find it? Then we took it off when you rode me reverse-cowgirl style?"

Her face goes red and her mouth parts open. "Knox," she mutters a warning. "This is why we can't be seen together. You are insanely inappropriate." Her amusement with me is barely there, only a hint in her glare.

A slow song comes on and the lights reflect in a circle, causing a glow to hit Madison every few seconds. She focuses her attention on the couples forming to sway to a solid choice of music.

Standing side by side with her, I play my part and look on too.

I speak without looking at her. "Having fun?"

Madison never went to prom; I know this because we talk about a lot of things when most of our relationship lately has been via text—the modern love letter.

"I thought it may have been fun to do this tonight, but the

whole night my colleagues have been sacrificing me like a lamb every time we need to check if a student is getting out of line." She sounds somber but softly smiles when she sees one of the jocks ask a girl who was sitting alone to dance. Madison quickly glances at me. "This is a horrible idea, you being here."

"No, it's not. I don't want to follow your plan anymore."

"Knox, what is this?"

"Me telling you that I can't hide it anymore, you and me, everything between us is too good." My hands fill my pockets as I look forward at the scene in front of us. I step to my side, enabling my shoulder to brush with Madison's, the touch alone magnifying a feeling that I can't seem to shake.

I notice her chest move up and down as she is either panicking or trying to calm down.

"I want to dance with you right here and now, then kiss you for the world to see."

Her gaze shoots in my direction. "Are you kidding me right now?" She seems slightly pissed. "Knox, this is *not* the time for this. Look around, these kids deserve all the attention on them, your sister included."

I can only grin to myself as we both look forward, standing casually, attending to our duty, but we both feel the connection between us, an overbearing tension. "You are really hot when you're feisty, more beautiful than normal."

"Do not throw charming words at me," she warns.

We both grow silent as we take in the scene of young love in front of us. Couples forming, couples probably soon ending, all believing their first love is the only love they will ever know.

And I want to scream at them all that it doesn't matter, because the best love is the kind you never saw coming.

"I don't want to wait, Madison. Be angry at me, but it's my timeline now," I inform her, very certain.

"Knox," her voice goes soft.

"You can be frustrating sometimes, but I follow willingly."

"What are you trying to say?" she whispers as both of us continue with our gaze forward.

"You're beautiful."

"Okay, so?" She is getting impatient.

"You make me feel things."

"You mentioned once." Her breath goes heavy.

My sight turns to her, and with the light casting a shadow on her face, she's the picture of a future I want. "And I wasn't going to wait to tell you that I love you."

Her head immediately whips in my direction with a smile forming on her face. We both look at one another with recognition, but she doesn't throw her arms around me because she straightens and looks behind me.

"Oh, Knox." Helen looks at me, surprised, then between Madison and myself.

Madison still seems out of sorts, as she seems frozen and blinks a few times. I volunteer the information. "Filling in for Grayson," I state as my eyes look between the two ladies.

"Sure, dear." Helen plays along then turns her attention to Madison. "Sorry, but Beal is asking if you can check the ladies' room. It seems we have a young lady in tears. Beal thinks you are more relatable, as you are younger, and I may agree."

Madison opens her mouth and tries to gather some

words, as I clearly threw her off with my declaration. "Right, I should probably do that."

As Helen walks away, I quickly grab Madison's arm before she can get far.

"This may be a while. Meet me at my place later?" she requests, and I hear it in her voice, see it in her eyes that I swear twinkle. Our night isn't over.

Leaning against her front door, I watch Madison slowly emerge from the apartment stairwell with her eyes fixed on me.

"You survived?" I ask, handing her a corsage. "Figured you never got one of these since you didn't do the prom-night thing."

She takes the flowers and gives me a knowing grin. "Steal them?"

I slant a shoulder up. "May have done an exchange, don't ask for what."

"Please tell me it's not…"

I remind her of a fact, "They are all mostly eighteen, so yeah, their night is extra heightened where they live in the moment, young, free, and gloved up."

Her face looks horrified. "You gave out condoms?"

"Wait, what? No, I'm not *that* irresponsible of a chaperone. It was mints."

She ruefully shakes her head and puts her key in the door. Then she pauses and looks at me, with her head tilted and her smile forming as the door opens, and she must have left a light on somewhere in her place because I can see her outline enough. "You... mentioned something earlier—"

Grabbing her arm, I drag her inside and close the door behind us. I yank her to me, pulling our bodies flush. My hands capture her face to cradle as I dip my head down and slam my lips down on hers.

Then, like a crazed man, I need to make it clear that I'm claiming her.

"I love you," I remind her.

Madison smiles with swollen lips. "I was hoping for that confirmation."

Backing her against the door, I don't care, and I grab hold of the fabric of her dress along her shoulder, tugging it down harshly, causing it to rip. My lips make up for it by kissing the curve of her shoulder, creating a trail up her neck in hurried kisses.

"I love you, Knox," she breathes out right before my mouth returns to her own.

My hand slides up her leg to take hold of her panties and then I'm tearing them down without much grace. Her fingers fumble with the buttons of my shirt as our mouths stay glued together.

Turning her in one quick move, her back is against my front, and I know she has a mirror next to her front door which we now stare into.

My teeth tease and nip up to her ear as I pull her hair to the side, maybe a little too roughly, but she moans. "Look in the mirror." Our eyes lock via the reflection. "See? This is what you look like as mine. You're the one I love, and you love me," I murmur into her ear as my hands coast along her body, encouraging her arms to come up and hook behind my neck, displaying her body, giving me access to treat her like a canvas.

She coos and her body arches away from me as my hand slides between her legs. "I'll follow you until we don't need to worry, but the moment that day comes, then you better believe that everyone will know that you're mine. Do you understand?"

She nods gently, as my finger swirls against her clit must be causing her to lose focus.

"Maddie."

"Yes," she rasps. "I understand."

My other hand drags the fabric of the no-longer-fitted dress to the side to cup her breast.

"But tonight, and every other night, you follow my lead."

She chortles a laugh and her brows raise. "Oh, is that a challenge?"

Releasing my hands, I spin her body around and pin her wrists above her head against the door. "You better damn believe it."

Madison tries to capture my mouth with her own, but I play with her by retreating, dancing with her lips.

Then we still for a second, taking in this moment.

"I love you," she softly whispers.

Unbuckling my pants, I'm a man completely high on contentment that I didn't know was possible. "I love you."

We kiss as I lower my pants, before I wrap my arms around her waist and hoist her up, trapped against the door and me, her legs locking around my middle.

Sliding into her, we both groan and moan from my ruthless first thrust to confirm our union.

Her back hits against the door on every pump, and a grunt escapes my lips as I reach impossible depths. Madison cries out my name as we move.

When I slip out, I release her legs and fall to my knees

to lick her along her slit. Her entire body curves against my mouth. But I only give her a few strokes before I'm back to standing and twisting her body around with palms landing against the door as I re-enter her.

"Knox," she pleads and presses against me, driving me crazy.

I lean over and her mouth meets my own when she glances over her shoulder.

Maybe I should go more gentle, but how can I when we've been chasing one another for months, forming a relationship that I'm never going to let go of? No, now, in this moment, I need to prove to her that she's the only thing I want, and all indications are that she feels the same, and if she didn't, then I wouldn't let her go without a fight.

She pants my name as I take us closer and closer, until we are tumbling into an orgasm in one another's arms, a disheveled mess against her front door, all because I didn't want to wait, because I love her. I fucking love her.

And Christ, she's beautiful in my arms, completely undone.

Our breaths merge as our heart rates sync, and we hold each other so close.

Her body is still trembling, and we fall to the floor, my arms wrapping around her tighter, keeping her close against my body. I kiss her hair, her cheek, every part that she offers in her state of ecstasy.

———

WE FINALLY MANAGED to make it to bed. Naturally, the night called for a slower session where I was a little less feral and proved to Madison that I have a soft sensual side that's only for her.

Lying in bed naked, Madison rests against my chest as I stroke her hair.

"We're almost there," she reminds me, and she means the calendar.

I roll my eyes. "Don't remind me."

Her fingers draw circles against my skin, and I love the feathery touch. "I'll go with you to visit your aunt and uncle," I say, as I remember she mentioned going next weekend. "It's out of town, doesn't count."

She playfully hits me and looks up. "I would love it, but I'm not sure they will be down with the sharing-a-bed thing."

I frown because the world isn't throwing us any favors. Blowing out a breath, I remind myself to be a respectable man. "Okay, what about getting a hotel nearby? That could be fun, do a little weekend roleplay."

She laughs before returning to resting against my body. "I'm not sure what you have in mind, but I may consider. It's just that I kind of like staying there at their farm, it's cozy. Just like Olive Owl."

Her answers warm me. Every. Single. Time.

"Remind me I love you. I can do this. We've gotten this far, so I can manage a little more time."

She tickles my navel and kisses my pec. "You can. Besides, now I have to listen to you." She moves to straddle me. "Every." Kisses my chest, moves down, feels promising... "Single." Going lower... "Time." She is just above the line, but close enough to make my cock crave being deep inside her mouth.

Madison throws me a cheeky look before sliding her mouth back up and returning to lie in my arms.

But I don't even care. Because she and I are something so damn good.

MADISON

L ooking at the students walking one by one across the stage to collect their diploma, a permanent smile graces my face. Gone is their youth and off to their adult life they all go. One day they will realize how precious this time was, but alas, they will probably only realize that later in life.

I pass Principal Beal rolled-up diplomas as she reads each name, one by one; every whistle and hoot still surprises us in a unique way each time. And we ruefully shake our heads when a student takes out their cell phone for a selfie on stage, even though we asked them not to bring phones. They aren't exactly in a position to listen anymore, as they can no longer be expelled.

And when the moment comes for Lucy's name to be called, I do my best to stay composed. It's hard to do when I look out into the audience and see her three older brothers looking at her with such affection and admiration. I swear I even see Grayson wipe a tear away. Meanwhile, Bennett and Knox clap and whistle, and of course Knox decides to set off a paper confetti cannon, to which Lucy covers her face in slight embarrassment.

But this moment is all of theirs. Each one of her brothers felt a responsibility to her and wanted to carry her into adulthood. Not just at the request of their father, but also because they are big brothers hyped up on love and pride for their sister.

I look at Lucy in her gown and hat approaching Beal.

"Congratulations, Lucy." Beal passes her the diploma and shakes her hand.

"Thank you," Lucy replies as they both turn to the photographer for a photo.

Lucy then steps forward a few steps to shake my hand. I flash my eyes at her, a sort of secret sign that I'm more connected to her than all the other graduates. Not just because of Knox, but also, because she is one of my favorite students, and I swear it isn't bias.

"I'm no longer in high school," she tells me so only I can hear.

"No, you're not," I confirm with a bright smile.

We continue to shake hands as the room claps.

Lucy steps closer. "Thank you for loving him."

My face freezes when I look at her.

"I would hate to be leaving if he was alone. But Knox has something good happening, and it's with you."

I continue to smile and shake her hand. "Lucy," I mutter without letting my smile falter.

"Relax, no more sentimental crap. Besides, a wise teacher once told me that when I am no longer in high school, I should go for things." She flashes her eyes at me before walking away, and I know she is warning me that her eyes are still set on a bad idea.

But I can only gently shake my head with my smile

fixed because Lucy may just set fires one day, and that's better than sitting behind a rock.

The rest of the ceremony goes by quickly, as does the punch and cookies in the library afterward, where parents are constantly coming to me to say thanks. I don't get any opportunity to approach the Blisswood clan, even though I feel Knox's eyes on me the entire time. But I will see them all at Lucy's graduation dinner.

Helen waves a hand at me and indicates for me to come to the decorated cookie table that the booster club arranged. Knowing I don't have much choice, I take a deep breath, and with my head held high, I arrive to Helen unwrapping a fresh plate of sprinkled cookies.

"Hi, Helen."

"Be a dear and help me unwrap the gluten-free brownies." She indicates to another plate.

I get to work and come to her aid, but it only takes a few seconds into my recruitment for my eyes to shoot up when Helen says something. "What was that?" I double-check that I heard her correctly.

"You and Knox can now get frisky in front of everyone, and we can't even bat an eyelash," she says as she arranges the cookie plate.

My tight-lipped smile stays as my eyes go wide, and I quickly search the room to ensure nobody heard. "Helen, what would make you say that?"

She throws a cookie onto a plate and looks at me. "Really, dear? I know everything, plus I'm at Olive Owl more than most. While Knox plays it cool, he has been unusually happy as of late, and that can only be explained by a young lady casting him under her spell. And since my booster club set-up, then I will only assume that I'm *solely* responsible."

"Solely?"

She waves a paper plate in the air. "Why else would you be together? Anyway, I've done my best to curb the gossip at the meetings, but now I'm relieved that's behind us with Lucy off to college. Some of those moms pull out their claws for intel. Now I'm free to express with everyone that we are all happy to see those boys settling down."

"So I keep hearing." I deadpan.

My head scans the room for Knox, and our eyes catch as he stands holding a cup of punch talking with Coach Dingle. He gives me an inquisitive look, and I indicate my head to Helen, and his response is a wince. I'm sure he knows I'm getting my ear chewed off.

But no public displays or declarations today, as this is the students' afternoon. Later will be a different story.

———

Arriving at Lucy's graduation dinner at Olive Owl, and I'm free to do what I want with Knox from this moment forward.

Walking to the back patio that Kelsey and Brooke decorated, I see them setting up for the BBQ.

"Hi, ladies, can I help with anything?" I ask as I set my bag down and look down at the toddler crawling on a blanket.

Kelsey leans over the table, pouring a bag of chips into a bowl. "I think we have everything under control. Grayson and Bennett are gathering BBQ supplies from the shed, Rosie is…" Kelsey looks at Brooke.

"Rosie should be here." Brooke looks around. "Rosie!" she calls out then looks to Kelsey and me. "She was with the dog a minute ago."

"Pretzel," I call out.

A few seconds later, we hear a woof, followed by Rosie giggling and running after the dog.

"Where did you go?" Brooke asks her daughter before returning to the salad she's tossing.

"Sorry, Mommy, I was with Uncle Knox."

"Oh, this is trouble," Brooke mumbles then smiles sweetly at her daughter. "And where is Uncle Knox?"

Rosie blushes when she looks at me then back at her mom. "I'm supposed to tell Madison to go somewhere."

"Oh yeah? Where would that be?" Kelsey asks.

Rosie points in the direction of the path where she came from.

"The swing?" I ask, amused.

She nods her head.

Kelsey and Brooke give me knowing eyes.

"I guess I shall go there." I point in the direction of the path and can't control my curious smile.

I actually haven't been to the tree swing since all those months ago when Knox and I were two people getting to know one another very reluctantly. But as I step on every stone and push tall grass out of the way, I emerge to find Knox leaning against the tree with a swaggered look.

"Hey there." I stop and can't control the grin spreading on my face.

He steps forward to kiss me, with his hands running to the back of my neck to bring me closer to him, to not let go, not now and maybe not ever. I murmur a sound as his tongue sweeps into my mouth to meet my own.

He pulls away, nearly breathless. "Hey."

Our noses touch for a second, before he steps back, taking my hand in his and guiding me to the swing. "I believe from this moment on, no rules."

I sit down and he pushes me gently. "The calendar does indicate that, yes."

"It's also summer vacation for you."

"Thankfully. I need a break from teenage angst and fictional men," I quip.

He chuckles softly before circling around and kneeling down to enable us to be at eye level as he holds the ropes of the swing. "I was thinking we could go to Vegas."

I do a double take to try and study his face. He isn't joking. "Uhm?"

He laughs. "No, not for that."

"Oh, then why would you like to go to Las Vegas in the middle of the summer when it's like a gazillion degrees there?" I ask as my legs gently nudge him while I swirl on the swing.

"There is air conditioning, smart one, and this hot teacher I met once mentioned if she was ever in Vegas then she would get a tattoo, and I know you've been thinking about it," Knox explains, and I connect the dots of where his question came from.

"Ooh, this is a wild kind of Vegas trip." I'm completely on board.

"You have no idea what ideas are swimming in my head right now." His tone is pure trouble. "Bring a bikini," he growls before he kisses the curve of my neck.

"I will consider it," I taunt him. "Wait, was this a question or a you-already-planned-a-trip kind of statement?"

"We leave next weekend, then I'm back for a week before taking Lucy on her graduation trip," he explains.

My mouth opens but no words come out. "Okay, I'm on board."

"Good." He bops my nose with his finger.

We stay there for a good minute, just looking at one

another and kissing necks, corners of mouths, and lips. Until he pulls back and looks at me with serious eyes.

"You okay?" I ask, clearly amused and confused.

Our locked gaze breaks when we hear Pretzel's collar, and soon we have a dog breaking our embrace. He is slobbering more than usual, as it's a warm day out.

"You should get him a baby pool for the summer. I mean, I know you have the pond, but the baby pool seems like it may be less intimidating for him, plus it'll keep him cool," I mention as I pet Pretzel's head.

"You can get whatever you want for here. In fact, make it your home."

My eyes peer up from Pretzel's fur to Knox's face who looks mighty sure. "What do you mean?" I ask.

His head bobs side to side. "Move in with me," he states more than he asks.

"As in here at Olive Owl?" I try to wrap my head around this idea.

"Yeah, here. Move in while I'm away with Lucy. Then when I return, it's you and me. Collect eggs with me in the mornings, taste grapes that may or may not be ready, garden whatever the hell you want, stay in my bed every night. Move in with me."

Pretzel makes a whimpering noise, and I see he is wagging his tail. "Should I be concerned he seems to understand everything of this conversation?"

"Who cares. He wants you here too."

"Does this mean I get to become a co-parent to Pretzel?"

Knox snickers. "You already were, in case you didn't notice."

"You want me to move in with you?" I ask again as I consider how I feel about this.

I have no hesitations. I had an inkling that this would be our next step, and I'm over the moon that I get to be with Knox, living together under the same roof.

"Yes, shortcake, now will you stop stalling and just confirm that we are going to drive one another crazy on the holy grounds of Olive Owl?" He isn't patient.

I propel off the swing to stand and look down at Knox who is still kneeling down and desperately waiting. I begin to speak but stop. This is too fun. I try again then pause. His jaw goes slack.

"Yes?" he urges.

"No—"

"What do you mean no?" His voice cracks and panic floods across his face.

"No, that's not what I mean," I attempt to stop him.

He stands up with urgency. "You said no again."

"I'm trying to say yes!" I shriek.

"Yes? But you said no!"

We both stand in front of one another, charged. "I was saying, 'No, Knox, you shouldn't assume, but yes, in this case you are right.' Of course I want to live with you, and it's the perfect step for us."

I walk into his arms that come to wrap around my body.

"So you were saying yes?" He's still unsure.

I playfully slap his shoulder. "Yes!"

"Fuck, be more direct next time, okay?" he scolds me before he grins and kisses me, tipping me back in the process.

My hands come to hold his face in place. "Sure. How about let's go celebrate your sister's graduation, and then when everyone leaves, you can fuck me so deep and hard that I won't be able to walk for days, which is completely okay, since I'm on vacation, so I can recover in peace. Direct enough?"

"Works for me." He kisses me again before taking my hand and walking us back to the main house.

But I stop him for a second by yanking his hand. "Hey, Knox, did you ask me here because this is a special spot?" I hear the softness in my tone.

His jaw ticks. "Yeah. Yeah, I did."

Everything about this is right. The sensitivity of it, his swoony look, and the fact that it's special to him and he's sharing it with me.

"I love you, Knox," I remind him.

"And I love you, clearly. Now let's go eat." He tows me back toward his family and the place I can now call home.

EPILOGUE: KNOX

3 YEARS LATER

Walking into the kitchen after checking the fencing out in the field, I inhale in the smell of fresh dill. I admire the scene in front of me of Madison in shorts, a tank top, and focused on making lunch while Pretzel stands at attention next to her, hoping for scraps, knowing he always gets one.

"A tomato is ready," I say as I hold up the red fruit from the garden.

She looks up at me and smiles. "Hey, trouble. Chicken salad today. Helen has the guests taken care of, and then it's quiet for a few days. I'm going to Kelsey's later to help with the kids; I can't imagine having a preschooler and a newborn." Madison shudders and inside I do too because Bennett just welcomed another baby and looks beyond exhausted. More so than Grayson, who also has a toddler running around, plus an eight-year-old who acts like a princess.

It's July, summer, my favorite time of year. I get extra

time with my wife, and the Illinois heat makes her extra sensual, and I love it.

I wrap my arms around her from behind and kiss the little tattooed book on her shoulder blade, the ink she chose in Vegas while buzzed on vodka and cranberry. It was a fun night, a wild night. She insisted we have sex, but she wasn't allowed to lie on her plastic-covered tattoo. The positions we tried were both classic and adventurous. Then she moved to Olive Owl a few weeks later.

One year later, we returned to Vegas and eloped. Drove my family crazy because they missed out. But truthfully, we didn't plan it. We went back for another tattoo and instead decided on a whim to skip the tattoo and get married instead.

Pulling Madison close to my body, I inhale the smell of her hair, a mix of chocolate and honey because she baked last night. "Happy two-year anniversary," I whisper.

She glances over her shoulder and gives me a suspicious look. "Did the calendar app remind you or you're that crazy about me?"

I snicker at her joke. "Of course I know which day we got married."

"Mmm, okay." She pretends to still doubt me before she places some potato chips on a plate. "How about you get a coffee, a *strong* coffee."

Uh-oh, that's a bad sign.

"Uhm, everything okay?" I ask as I make my way to the table and grab a mug on the way.

"Totally fine. I mean, well, you know I had that appointment this morning, right?"

Ah, the baby thing. We've been in no rush, but then a few months ago Madison suggested maybe we could try. And admittedly, my nieces and nephews weakened my baby resolve, and when your wife asks to try for a baby when she is on her knees, then your mouth spins out a *totally*.

So here we are on the baby-making express… just not going as fast as the normal Blisswood myth would presume it would go. And we are completely relaxed about that. Madison went to the doctor this morning for a checkup, something to do with cycles or something. She insisted it was a woman-only appointment.

She smiles sweetly as she sets a plate in front of me at the kitchen table then sits across from me. Her knees come up to her chest as she takes a large sip of iced tea from her glass and watches me.

Taking a bite of my sandwich, I'm in heaven. Caffeine, protein, and a beautiful woman. What more could a man need?

Her head indicates to the small square box lying on the table.

"What's this?" I flop my sandwich down and grab the box.

"You see, it was a normal appointment, well, was supposed to be, but it turns out that it wasn't needed because…" She's acting nervous, and a smile plays on her lips as she watches me.

"We… we're already… pregnant?" I croak out what I can assume is what she is indicating.

"No, well, yes, I mean…"

"Now isn't the time to do that not-clear-answer-debating thing," I deadpan.

"Look in the box," she urges.

Opening the box and I see it right away, a photo. One of those ultrasound photos.

"We're pregnant," she rasps and cries. "But there isn't just one…"

My eyes see the two dots with A and B pointing to each one.

My stomach flips and my heartrate quickens. "Shit, twins?" I can't pinpoint why I'm not more overwhelmed by the thought, but then I realize this is probably what they call shock, as I can't process what this will all mean, and probably won't until it wears off.

"Yeah, some bullseye, huh?" she attempts to joke, but I think she is still in disbelief from all this too.

It's a long minute or two of silence. A calming silence, albeit a silence.

"It's a joke, right? I mean, we are having one baby." I hold up a finger. She leans over and unhooks another one of my fingers until I hold up the number two.

"Two babies," she repeats.

My fingers return to the number one. "One baby."

She corrects my hand again. "Two," she chirps out.

Then I look at her and the grin can't help emerging. "Wasn't expecting this."

This has to be karma.

I'm the uncle that my siblings know can only handle kids in mini-doses. And yes, I could see a junior me or Madison in the future… but that was *one*, I signed up for one kid!

"It's still really early, which is why I didn't even know, but my hormone levels in the bloodwork were really high, which made the doctor check with an ultrasound," Madison explains.

Quickly I reach out to her hands and encourage her to come sit on my lap.

"Good thing we have space here," I quip.

"Yeah, I want to raise them here. I know we are a bit out of town, but this is where our life is." She always says the right things.

I kiss her and then kiss her again. God, I love this woman.

"Well, this is going to take a few hours to wrap my head around, but I am happy," I assure her.

She smiles in response, but our moment is interrupted by the sound of Bennett and Grayson storming into the room, with Drew in tow.

"We need to talk," Bennett states as he heads to the coffee pot. He's the calmest out of all my siblings, yet he's still unimpressed by something.

Grayson and Drew both look to be in deep thought and on edge.

"Can you give me a minute?" Drew implores as he rakes a hand through his hair.

"Fine, then let's talk about this and lay down the damn truth." Grayson's tone is sharp, which isn't like him at all.

Madison looks at me for a clue, and I shrug my shoulders.

"What brings everyone to Olive Owl on this fine day?" I greet them all, unamused, as right now I should be basking in the news I just discovered. Madison slides off me and returns to her chair. Our celebration will have to wait.

"We discovered some intel that needs to be shared and discussed," Bennett informs me before taking a sip of his coffee.

I hold a hand up. "Okay, but can we chill out? Because my brain can't process too much right now."

I need to focus on the news my wife just shared.

"Him and her. Them," Grayson states with a steely look.

"Them who?" I ask as I throw a morsel of a chip into my mouth to pep me up a little.

"Knox, I can explain." Drew seems to be promising me something.

Looking between everyone, I'm lost. "Clue me the fuck in. Why would I care about 'them'? Is this about Drew with some girl?"

Bennett chuckles almost sarcastically. "Oh man, here we go," he mutters.

Grayson shakes his head. "Because that *some girl...*?" His eyes go wide as if I should know.

I look between my brothers and then at my wife, who seems to have figured it out before me, because her mouth gapes open and her hand comes to cover her mouth.

My heart, already pulsing fast from the news of my impending fatherhood, drops even lower into my stomach, if that's possible.

I look at Drew, then my brothers, then back at Drew. It dawns on me that someone is home for the summer.

"Lucy," I manage to seethe out.

"Bingo," Bennett adds in his commentary.

Grayson and I both look at one another with heated eyes, a recognition that this is our biggest fear coming alive.

"You're sleeping with my little sister?" I manage to ask the question and not blink.

Who the hell decided that this would be my day today? One bombshell after another.

"It's not what you think," Drew attempts to justify something, I have no idea what.

I stand up out of my chair, ready... for what, I'm not

sure. How *do* I feel about this? Drew is a way better choice than that nerdy guy Lucy dated a while back. And Drew is halfway in age between Lucy and me, but he's my friend, our friend, a sort of honorary brother. He knows the code.

Looking at my bothers, I know one of us is about to lose their cool. I just don't know if it's me, because how do I feel about this?

"Then you better explain, and fast," I order.

ACKNOWLEDGMENTS

Thank you for reading Something Good. Enemies to lovers always takes us on a journey. I loved writing Madison and Knox too. These books wouldn't be possible without readers like you!

Thanks to Lindsay, my editor, you make it such a joy to write. I look forward to every e-mail.

To Brittni, for always reading the very early *rough* stages.

To Eric, Christopher, and Kate you cover magicians you all are!

My ARC team and bloggers who share. You rock! Pure and simple.

I owe thanks to my music playlist, ginger shots, and my husband wrangling in our offspring. We survived yet again…

Made in the USA
Middletown, DE
08 July 2022